HALLOWEEN BEYOND

PIERCING THE VEIL

LISA MORTON, LUCY A. SNYDER, AND KATE MARUYAMA

Book 4 in Crystal Lake's Dark Tide series

Let the world know:
#IGotMyCLPBook!

Crystal Lake Publishing
www.CrystalLakePub.com

WELCOME
TO ANOTHER

CRYSTAL LAKE PUBLISHING
CREATION

Subscribe to Crystal Lake Publishing's Dark Tide series for updates, specials, behind-the-scenes content, and a special selection of bonus stories - http://eepurl.com/hKVGkr

THE TALKING-BOARD

LISA MORTON

KAYLA STRUGGLED TO push down the poisonous dread that erupted as she re-read the message on her phone:

Halloween party tonight. You coming? Don't forget costume.

She knew she was the main reason Sophie was hosting this party It was all about trying to take her mind off the one-year anniversary of Hailey's disappearance, just for a few hours.

Kayla also knew it wouldn't work. A party of loud, clumsy college kids getting drunk wasn't going to make her forget what had happened to her sister. Or what *hadn't* happened: she hadn't come home after Halloween last year.

Still, Sophie was her bestie, and an eternal optimist who always believed she could help. Everyone, Kayla included, thought Sophie was on track to be a great leader, even a politician if she could survive that career's cynical pitfalls. When Kayla's dad had split after Hailey was born, Sophie had been there for her, precociously wise for a nine-year-old. Kayla would go to the party to support Sophie, not for any other reason.

She sighed as she glanced at the time; it was two o'clock now. She had six hours and zero ideas to come up with a costume. Last year she hadn't dressed up or gone out. She'd been at home in torn jeans and ghoulish make-up handing out candy to trick or treaters while their mother, Jess, had been stuck at work, and Hailey had been . . .

No. Stop it. Besides, today's only the 29ᵗʰ, so it's not really the anniversary. Not yet.

Kayla swiped on her phone, going to social media instead, trying to lose herself in the mindless chatter of her friends. She scrolled quickly past her own posts, which always seemed dowdy ("Making cookies") and unimaginative compared to her friends. There was Sophie, flashing grins and hand gestures, her dark skin standing out against a row of glowing ghosts in her front yard. Rosita had yet another selfie of herself looking adorable, baring that toned, bronze midsection she was so proud of. Under her mop of scarlet hair, Katt was making sad faces, upset that her favorite singer hadn't advanced on *AGT*. Danielle modeled a kitten costume she'd be wearing tonight, her black hair crowned with fluffy ears, her perfect cleavage busting a tight, striped corset. She'd added a hashtag to her post: *#halloweenbeyond*.

Kayla had seen that come up in a few other posts; curious, she typed it into the search bar. There were tens of thousands of people all over the country using the tag, raving about this pop-up Halloween store that had suddenly appeared in their towns. Photos of some of the locations showed a hip retail spot with walls lined in costumes, aisles of decorations, and shelves of party goods. The costumes didn't seem to be the same run-of-the-mill crap based on whatever television show was popular three months ago The headstones and skeletons and animatronics all had rave reviews.

There was one right here in Red Creek, less than ten minutes away. Kayla knew it was likely to be jammed on the last Saturday before Halloween, but it was her best shot at getting a costume.

She found Jess in the backyard, pulling out dead corn stalks. It was good to see her mother doing something she enjoyed instead of working at the restaurant she managed. Kayla sometimes felt guilty about how little household money she contributed by tutoring, but Jess insisted that she not take a harder job. "You just focus on college for now," she'd told her. "You'll pay me back when you're a doctor."

Until last year, Kayla had also looked after her twelve-year-old sister while Mom was at work.

"Hey," she said, "looking good out here." Their backyard was small, but Jess had transformed it into a tiny Eden, with a luxurious mix of flowering annuals, natives, vegetables, and herbs. The upstate New York winter was coming, though, and it was time to prepare for the cold, barren months ahead.

The gardener looked up, smiling, removing a gardening glove to wipe a stray lock of graying hair from her forehead. Glancing around, she answered, "Wait until you see it next spring. Hailey would have . . . " She trailed off, looking away, and Kayla realized yet again that as hard as this was on her, it was worse on her mother. After all, Kayla had lost a sister, but Jess had lost a *child*.

"I'm sorry," Jess said, her gaze unfocused now, fingers curling in, "I just . . . it's the time of year . . . "

"I know." Kayla was never sure what to do with these small breakdowns—offer a hug, a memory, a reassurance? She envied

Sophie's natural people skills, how she always knew the right thing to say or do. Kayla wanted to heal and help—it's why she was in Pre-Med at RHU—but she'd always felt clumsy, an outsider.

At last Kayla said, in a voice barely above a whisper, "I think about her all the time, too. Especially now."

After a second, Jess rose, tossed her gloves and hat aside, and gripped her first (and now last) daughter's shoulders, looking into her eyes. "We'll get through this, okay? You and me."

They embraced then, Kayla feeling some of her mother's natural strength flowing into her. When they pulled apart, Kayla asked, "Are you sure you're fine with me going to Sophie's party tonight?"

Jess nodded. "It'll be nice to have a rare night to myself. I've got plans with a cheap bottle of wine and whatever's on Netflix."

Laughing, Kayla said, "Oh my God, my mom's a lush." She started to turn away, then remembered why she'd come out here. "I need a costume for Sophie's party tonight, and I heard about a great new store over on Second. Okay if I take the car? I should be back in less than an hour."

"Sure, honey. What are you going to be?"

"I've got absolutely no idea. I'm hoping inspiration will strike. Do you need anything while I'm out?"

Jess shook her head. "I'll do the main shopping later. You go ahead."

Kayla was almost in the house when Jess called after her, "Kayla . . . try not to spend too much on the costume."

She saw the pain the reminder caused her mother and replied, "I won't."

Turning, Kayla paused when she heard her name called again, although this time the voice was soft, quiet, barely audible. Looking back at Jess, she asked, "Yeah, mom?"

Jess peered at her blankly.

"Did you say something?"

"No."

"Oh. I thought I heard . . . " Kayla shrugged it off then and headed for the house, trying to put aside the instant aside.

The voice had sounded like Hailey's.

THE TALKING-BOARD

OCTOBER 29TH, 2:30 P.M.

As Kayla had suspected, the Halloween Beyond store was chaos. Long orange banners with the store's logo—the name surrounded by a black, leafless tree, a red-eyed owl peering from the branches—covered the walls inside and out. Shoppers, including friends from college and neighbors, carried plastic baskets full of packaged costumes and fake bones, stopping as they pulled out their phones for photo ops. Video monitors overhead played colorful ads showing kids gasping as they encountered the store's animatronic Grim Creeper or Jack Pumpkindead figures; fog, spilling out of cleverly hidden machines, shrouded the floor.

Kayla stumbled back, startled, as a three-foot-long spider leapt at her from a corner, emitting a grating buzz before retreating slowly back into position, ready to spring at the next unwary customer. She made her way past the children's costumes (*don't look*, she commanded herself, hoping to avoid seeing something that reminded her of Hailey), heading for the adult women's section. Scanning quickly past the "sexy" costumes (she didn't feel up to *that* this year), she finally settled on a cute but not too revealing red devil costume. A plastic pitchfork completed the outfit. She thought Mom wouldn't find the total price too objectionable.

She was heading for the front when a display of party goods caught her eye. There, nestled in between the signs with "Wanted" ads for notorious slashers and the fleecy throw blankets sporting horror movie posters, were boxed games touted as "talking-boards." Curious, she pulled one out and examined it. It was essentially a Ouija board without the brand; a description on the back of the box claimed it was based on the "first device used to talk to the dead." Kayla doubted that bit of hyperbole, but she liked the design of the thing, which featured an ornate, retro font.

"Interesting, eh?"

Kayla looked up to see a store employee in a bright orange apron with a nametag reading "Maeve" standing a few feet away, smiling at her. The woman had almost-white, blonde hair, skin so pale that Kayla assumed it was very good make-up, and a face that impossibly suggested both youth and age.

"Oh," Kayla said, feeling awkward as she returned the box to the shelf, "it is. I've never heard of a 'talking-board'."

The woman peered at her for a second with deep green eyes that made Kayla feel as if she were being drowned in an overgrown creek. "Well," the clerk—Maeve—said, "those are fun, but they're a little expensive. I've got a cheaper one that's just missing the box, if you're interested."

Kayla was about to say "no" when she stopped to consider: it might be fun to have at the party. She remembered a birthday party— her seventh—when she and Sophie and a few other friends had found a Ouija board stashed in the back of a closet and had played with it until they'd gotten too scared. If she brought this to the party, she knew Sophie would laugh. Then they'd play it, and be reminded of a more innocent time, when things as minor as this had scared them.

"I might be interested," she said.

The clerk beckoned. "I've got it back here. Come on."

Did she have a hint of accent, something British, or . . . ? Kayla couldn't quite place it, but she followed as Maeve led the way through a door marked "EMPLOYEES ONLY."

The door swung shut behind them, instantly sealing Kayla away from the fog and the clamor. She followed the clerk past a break room, restroom, and storage until she stood beside an unmarked door and pulled out keys. As she went through them, a large object almost hidden away at the far end of the hallway caught her attention: it looked like an ancient tree, an oak, with gnarled bark and twisting branches. *It's just papier-mâché*, Kayla thought, *but it looks so real*. She was on the verge of walking to the tree when Maeve unlocked the door, flipped a light switch inside, and gestured Kayla in.

There was nothing special about this room—the usual stark overhead fluorescent lights, walls lined with steel shelving—but Kayla couldn't contain a shudder. She felt a heaviness in her chest, as if she'd been buried under oppressive earth. When she'd experienced this sensation in the past, it had always been accompanied by a voice no one else heard, or a moving shadow disappearing into the corner of a room. Kayla had sensed these things as long as she could remember, but at some point in childhood she'd learned not to talk about them, especially not after she'd heard Auntie Conn whisper something to Jess about how "you should consider getting her some help." After Hailey's disappearance, Kayla knew that Jess had deflected questions about what "the weird older sister" might have done.

Kayla realized the clerk was looking at her intently, those verdant eyes narrowed slightly in appraisal before turning away to pull an item from an upper shelf. "Here you are."

What she handed to Kayla looked slightly like the talking-boards for sale in the store, but it was obviously older—*far* older—and made of solid wood instead of cheap pressboard. It was simpler, with just letters and numbers arrayed in three rows across its surface, no cute wily-looking moon or serene sun; the only complete words were "yes" and "no", in the upper corners. The planchette was also real wood (oak, Kayla guessed), and had three metal pins extruding an inch below the bottom where the modern versions had little plastic knobs.

"What *is* this?" Kayla asked. "I mean, it looks kind of like the other ones, but . . ."

"It came in a case with the regular shipment, but . . . well, we think it was probably a return and was sent to us by mistake."

Kayla knew this piece was no simple return, but she stayed silent as she held it in her hands, examining it.

The planchette abruptly jerked and slid across the board, landing on "H."

"Whoa," said Maeve, "I think it wanted to say 'hello'."

Or, Kayla thought, *it wanted to spell out HAILEY.*

"How much is it?"

"Well, we can't sell it new, so we'll make it half the price of the boxed units. Sound good?"

As Kayla held the board, she could almost feel it vibrating in her hands, thrumming with some sort of cycled power. It scared her, but it also intrigued her; instinct told her she had to take it. She finally nodded, her throat dry.

Maeve walked her back to the sales floor and up to the front counter, where they bypassed the line. She whispered instructions to the young woman behind the cash register, Kayla's purchases were rung up, and Maeve said, "I hope it serves you well," before disappearing back into the mass of shoppers.

As Kayla paid, she hoped she hadn't just done something very, very wrong.

OCTOBER 29ᵀᴴ, 3 P.M.

When Kayla got home, she heard noises from the attic. Knockings, rustlings.

She froze for a few seconds, listening, then made her way down the hall, where she saw the attic ladder extended, the trapdoor in the ceiling open. Moving to the base of the ladder, Kayla looked up into the dark attic, calling out, "Mom?"

Jess appeared behind her, causing Kayla to jump. "Oh, sorry," Jess said, as she put out a hand to steady her daughter. "I was up in the attic looking for some Halloween stuff, but I found something else I don't think you've ever seen."

She handed Kayla an old book, pages bulging out with years of moisture, cloth splitting along the edges of the binding. Flipping it open, Kayla saw page after page of old-fashioned-looking handwriting. "What is this?"

"It belonged to several-times-great Aunt Hester—her diary." Jess took the journal, flipped through it briefly, handed it back opened to a specific page. "Read that. I think you'll get a kick out of it."

Kayla saw the book was opened to an entry dated October 31, 1892. "Oh, wow. Thanks—I'll take it into the living room."

She walked down the hallway, chose her favorite comfy chair, and sprawled there, opening the book in her lap.

October 31, 1892—Clara decided to hold a Hallowe'en party. Her family has an Irish maid, Siobhan, who told them all about the day and helped them arrange the party. Mother let me take the buggy to Clara's house, although our stable-hand David drove. The party started at 4 p.m. All of us had to enter Clara's house by stepping over witches' brooms placed across the threshold. Some of the girls found that quite startling, and squealed as they entered.

There were a dozen of us present, all girls I knew from church or school. We started the proceedings with some taffy-pulling, during which Sarah Mackenzie got quite sticky and made a mess of things. After we'd finished the candy, we moved into the living room, where we played games like tossing seeds into a pumpkin with its top removed.

Once the sun went down, we started telling our fortunes. We burned nuts by the hearth, naming each one for our various suitors and waiting to see which cracked first. We played a game that Siobhan called "luggie bowls", during which we were each blindfolded and then told to pick one of seven bowls positioned on the floor. Whichever we touched first foretold our future. I touched one full of water, which meant I'd be going on a long sea voyage. I do hope that's true, because I love the adventure of sailing.

Lastly, Siobhan told us ghost stories from her native Ireland, about ghosts and very mean fairies. Some of the girls got quite frightened, but most of us laughed and prodded each other when the stories were finished.

At about 10 p.m., David returned to collect me. Clara gave me some candy to take home, and I told her I'd had the most wonderful time. That night, as I crawled into my bed with the moonlight shining in through the window, I wished that the luggie bowls were right and I might have a great seagoing adventure in my life, although I realize it's ridiculous and un-Christian to believe in something learned from an old fortune-telling game. After all, there's no such thing as magic.

Having finished reading the Halloween entry, Kayla closed the book and set it aside, letting her mind drift, imagining that party from more than a century ago, and laughing as she wondered what Hester and Clara would have thought of a modern Halloween party. Kayla was sure they would have found it a scandalous affair indeed.

OCTOBER 29ᵀᴴ 8:10 P.M.

"You're here!" Sophie's hug filled Kayla with warmth, at least for a few seconds.

When they pulled apart, Sophie looked down at Kayla's costume. "Girl, you are rocking that devil style." Kayla did a small curtsey then stared at Sophie's gorgeous sexy witch outfit, which included a homemade black velvet pointed hat perched artfully atop her teased-out curls. "My devil bows before your witch."

She followed Sophie into the house, saying hi to other friends along the way. The strains of a remixed "Monster Mash" came from the living room; the decorations Kayla had glimpsed on Sophie's social media filled the house with jack-o'-lanterns, skeletons, and black cats. Sophie led the way into the kitchen, where she ladled dark red liquid out of a punch bowl into a cup that she put into Kayla's hand.

"What is it?" Kayla asked, eyeing the drink.

"Witches' brew," Sophie said in an ominous half-whisper, before adding, "okay, it's just punch made from a bunch of fruit juices, so it's even disgustingly healthy. Hey, what's in the bag?"

Kayla had forgotten she was still carrying the Halloween Beyond bag. "Check it out." She set down the punch and her pitchfork, opened the bag, and produced the talking-board and planchette.

"A Ouija board," Sophie said, eyeing it curiously, "but it doesn't look like other Ouija boards."

"The clerk at Halloween Beyond told me it's actually a talking-board and predates the Ouija board. She even sold me this one cheap because it came without a box."

Sophie hunched her shoulders, rubbed her hands together, and intoned in a grating, high voice, "We'll call some particularly nasty spirits, shall we?" Cackling, Sophie snatched the talking-board and planchette, heading for the living room. Kayla hesitated, trying to push down a pang of unease that had sprung up. *It's just a toy*, she told herself. *Besides, it's not even Halloween yet.*

Kayla looked up, startled to see Sophie eyeing her from the kitchen doorway. "You okay? Seemed like you kind of drifted off for a second."

Shrugging, Kayla said, "I'm . . . well, you know."

Sophie leaned against the door frame, her expression one of empathy. "Yeah, I do. I'm really glad you came tonight, though. I was afraid you wouldn't."

"I . . . " Kayla broke off, unsure how to say this She knew Sophie was skeptical about her brushes with the unseen, but she accepted it as part of Kayla. "I've been hearing her lately. A lot."

"Hearing her how? Like in dreams?"

"Well, that, too, but . . . no, I mean, like today at the Halloween Beyond store. The clerk took me into a backroom to show me that talking-board, and I thought it was going to spell out her name, like she was moving it."

Sophie walked up to her friend, put a hand on her shoulder.

"You knew the time around Halloween would be hard, right? I mean, I'd almost be surprised if you *weren't* having stuff like that happen."

"I suppose, but . . . Soph, this was so real."

Giving Kayla's arm a gentle tug, Sophie said, "Grab your pitchfork and come on out to the party. Maybe hearing Katt whine about how unfair the judges were this week on *America's Got Talent,* or whatever she's watching, will make you forget about Hailey for a few minutes."

Kayla nodded, allowed herself to be pulled out to the living room.

After an hour of idle chatter and munching roasted pumpkin seeds and sausages made to look like severed fingers, Kayla had almost forgotten about last year. She giggled as she watched Danielle model her kitten costume, flirted with a cute guy who was also pre-med (he'd even costumed himself in scrubs), spied Rosita not-so-secretly sharing a flask with a tall, gangly kid dressed as a Ghostbuster, and felt, for a change, almost like a normal twenty-year-old.

It was just after ten when Sophie entered the living room, pushed aside two others to make space for herself on the couch, and placed the talking-board on the coffee table. "Hey, look what Kayla brought."

The friends all crowded around, examining the device. "Is that a Ouija board?" Katt asked.

Kayla answered, "Kind of—it's called a talking-board, and I think this one might be really old."

"Ohh," Danielle said as she glanced mischievously around, "that means it's had lots of time to gather spirits."

A young man named Cole, who was dressed as a soldier and who Kayla had never met before tonight, said, "I don't think we should play with that thing. Ouija boards are gateways to evil shit. Do you guys know about Zozo?"

Sophie and Kayla exchanged a look before Sophie asked, "No. What's Zozo?"

The young man answered, "Not what—*who.* It's a demon that's called up by Ouija boards. It's really bad shit—makes threats, even carries through on some of them."

Sophie rolled her eyes. "You've seen too many horror movies." She rose, shut off the music, lit a candle on the table, and turned off all the lights in the room, plunging all but the faces closest to the board into darkness. Nodding at the planchette, she said, "I think there's room for about five fingers on there. Who wants to play?"

Katt bounced with excitement. "Me!" She stuck her right index finger on the planchette. Kyle, a gangly practical joker who was dressed as a dead businessman and was Danielle's off-and-on boyfriend, shoved his hand down, leaving Danielle to follow suit. Sophie added her finger before looking up at Kayla. "C'mon, you brought this, so you get to play."

Kayla tried to smile, but she was anxious. She hesitated before putting her finger on the planchette beside her friends'.

Danielle asked, "So what do we do now?"

Kyle replied, "We ask it stuff, like, you know—is Cole still a virgin?" Most of those present laughed, including Cole.

"No," Katt said, "we have to be serious about this. We start by asking if anyone's here."

The laughter stopped instantly, as all eyes turned to the board. After a few seconds, the planchette began to move, its motion seemingly aimless, circling the board.

"Who's doing that?" someone asked.

A reply came: "Kyle."

"I swear, I'm not!"

After a few more seconds of the slow, pointless movement, the planchette slid to "Yes".

"Yes," Katt breathed out, "there is a spirit present."

Looking down at the board, Sophie asked, "Can you tell us your name?"

The planchette went faster now, weaving a path up and down between the two rows of letters, spelling out B-U-N-N-Y.

Kayla went pale, gasping, "Oh my God."

Sophie looked up at her friend. "Isn't that what you used to call Hailey?"

Kayla could only nod.

Someone whispered, "Who's Hailey?"

Kayla barely heard the soft response: "Kayla's sister who died."

The planchette began to move forcefully now. I-M-N-O-T-

Sophie glanced at the others. "Kyle . . . "

"*It's not me.* Check it out." He removed his finger from the planchette. It continued to glide over the letters: -D-E-A-D.

Kayla jerked her hand away as if her fingers had been scalded. The remaining three followed suit; Sophie glared at Danielle and Katt. "Whichever one of you just did that, it wasn't funny."

Katt and Danielle both protested, but Kayla wasn't listening. She was getting to her feet, stumbling through the crowd of onlookers in the dark room. She heard Sophie's voice call out over the low murmur of voices, "Kayla, wait—"

Lights went on just as Kayla found the front door and yanked it open. Sophie followed her outside into the cool October night; when she caught Kayla's arm, Kayla turned to face her.

"That was fucked up," Sophie said, "but please don't leave."

"I'm pretty sure," Kayla responded, "that Katt, Danielle and Kyle never knew I called my sister 'Bunny'. Only you and I knew that."

Sophie's face fell. "You don't think I—"

Kayla cut her off. "No, I don't think you did it. That only leaves three other possibilities—that it was me, that it was Hailey, or that it was something pretending to be Hailey—and all of those freak me out, and I'm sorry, but I need to go home."

Nodding, Sophie pulled her into a hug. "I'm really sorry," She released her and added, "Call me tomorrow, okay? I'll be worried about you."

"Thanks. I will."

With that, Kayla turned and walked to her car, knowing that the night wasn't cool enough to cause her to tremble so violently.

OCTOBER 29ᵀᴴ, 11:25 P.M.

When Kayla came in, her mom was half-asleep on the couch, an empty wine glass nearby. "Oh, I thought you'd be home a lot later."

"I thought so, too, but . . . " Kayla hesitated, unsure what to say.

"Hailey?" Jess asked.

Kayla nodded, silent. Her mother sighed, said, "I know, baby. Me, too. I don't even remember what I just watched."

Turning away, Kayla was about to head for her own room when she stopped at the one closed door in the hallway.

Hailey's room.

She opened the door and stepped in, flipping on the light. She knew her mom came into the room from time to time, but Kayla hadn't been in here for nearly a year. She moved to the bed, made up with Hailey's purple comforter she'd loved, and sat down on the edge. There were Hailey's drawings of flowers and superheroes tacked up to a corkboard alongside the birthday card Dad had sent last year, there was her bookcase full of manga and fantasy novels, there was her desk with her laptop, her closet full of her brightly colored clothes. Kayla looked at all of it, letting her sister's personality fill her. She reached back to grab Mister Fluff, the teddy bear Hailey had loved since she was four, and hugged it tightly.

"Hailey," she whispered, looking around the room as if she'd find Hailey in it, "I don't understand. What did that mean?"

She waited. After a few seconds, she felt a weight on her chest, as if she'd just descended fifty feet into the ground. Sucking in air, she shivered as the temperature in the room fell. "Hailey?" she whispered.

She heard a rustling sound, turned her head just in time to see one of the drawings fall away from the bulletin board, drifting across the room to land at her feet.

It was a drawing of Kayla as a superhero, standing proud in a victorious pose. The ink outline was bold and sure, the coloring layered and vibrant, testament to the artist Hailey would surely have been as an adult.

"I don't . . . " Kayla felt tears on her face, but didn't release the toy bear to wipe them away. "Hailey, *make me understand.*"

The overhead light abruptly faded to a tiny yellow glow, just as a voice that was barely audible whispered in Kayla's ear, "*Save me.*"

Crying openly now, Kayla said, "How? How can I . . . "

The light flared back to full power, the temperature returned to normal, and Kayla's breathing eased.

Hailey was gone again.

OCTOBER 30TH, 7:00 A.M.

She dreamt of Hailey that night. She saw her sister at 12, then at 18, then at 24. She saw her as the young woman she would have, *should* have, become. Hailey, taller than Kayla, and pretty, almost ethereally so, standing in a glade of giant trees, dappled sun checkerboarding the soft, green moss underfoot. They were almost lucid dreams—Kayla experienced every detail, saw Hailey's hair and skin and the threads in the full-length green dress she wore, smelled the scent of ancient oaks, felt the sun where it touched her own skin, heard Hailey's soft breathing.

Breathing . . . "I'm not dead" . . .

In the dreamworld, Kayla tried to reach out to Hailey, but something seemed to separate them. Hailey smiled at her, but otherwise, she didn't speak or move. She gestured only once—to beckon. Kayla tried to step forward, but she couldn't.

When she awoke, as the sun came up, she remembered every detail of the dreams. She remembered . . . and she cried, in sheer frustration. She'd expected the one-year anniversary, this year's Halloween, to be bad, but she hadn't foreseen *this*.

Still, Kayla couldn't shake the idea that maybe Hailey really *was* alive, reaching out to her sister. They'd always had a strong bond, had been able to intuit what the other was thinking or doing. Last year on Halloween, Kayla had been shaken not by the sense that something had happened to Hailey, but rather that something had *not* happened. She knew that Hailey was not *there* anymore, not in Kayla's head where she'd always felt her.

When Kayla made her way out to the kitchen, Mom had already left to open the restaurant, leaving Kayla to her thoughts. As she made a morning cup of tea, she thought about everything that had happened since last night.

"Okay," she breathed out, and then thought, *What if Hailey is alive?*

At this point, a year later, no one really believed that—not the police, not their friends, not even Jess. That left only Kayla.

Taking the mug of Earl Grey into her bedroom, she logged into her laptop, ran a search for "Hailey Reynolds". She hadn't done this for months, and was surprised to see how much new material came up: a true crime podcast, blog entries, a Facebook discussion group. Kayla pored over all of it, inwardly wincing whenever her own name came up.

The facts hadn't changed. On Halloween night last year, Hailey had been at a party held by her friend Tisha Berry, who lived just a few hundred yards from a thick forest that had been known as the Ghost Woods for decades because it was supposedly haunted. At approximately 8:30 that evening, 12-year-old Darren Clepsky had dared anyone at the party to go into the Ghost Woods on Halloween night. Hailey, ever the fearless adventurer, had accepted; so had 13-year-old Josie Wang, who'd recently won a local martial arts tournament. They left the party shortly thereafter, headed for the Ghost Woods, using their phones as flashlights. Darren had been dressed as a pirate, Josie wore her black-belted gi, and Hailey was Princess Mononoke, the lead character in her favorite animated film, with an imitation fur costume and red stripes on her face.

Ninety minutes later, Darren and Josie returned to the party, covered in small scratches and looking stunned. Darren was missing his pirate captain's hat, Josie's gi was ripped and stained from stumbling against tree bark. Tisha's mother Diahann questioned the children, who seemed incapable of answering simple questions. Tisha remembered that they'd left with Hailey, who wasn't with them now. Tisha's father, Will, took a more powerful flashlight and headed into the Ghost Woods, calling Hailey's name. He searched for an hour before returning home. Diahann had treated the simple wounds Darren and Josie had acquired, which she guessed they'd obtained from running through the brush at some point. The two children had recovered enough to speak, but claimed to have no memory of anything from the time they'd entered the Ghost Woods.

The police were called, as was Jess. She and Kayla arrived at the Berry home before the police did; they immediately began their own search of the Ghost Woods, joined shortly thereafter by two policemen and Will Berry. The search continued until morning, but Hailey wasn't found. The police sent Kayla and Jess home for rest while they continued the search with dogs.

There was no trace of Hailey. Police began a serious investigation, calling on the community for witnesses, talking to anyone who lived around the Ghost Woods. At one point, their questions centered on Brigid Donnelly, a 74-year-old eccentric who lived by herself on a few acres of land at the western edge of the woods. Brigid, whose family had occupied this same plot since 1845, said she'd been out checking on a disturbance among her hens at about 9:45, but hadn't seen or heard anything.

Brigid was a suspect. So were Jess, Kayla, and the ever-popular anonymous psycho who lurked in the woods on a Halloween night, waiting for prey. A homeless man who'd been spotted in a nearby fast-food restaurant covered in blood at approximately 11:15 was found and questioned, but the blood turned out to be red wine he'd spilled on himself, and passersby recalled seeing him in front of the fast-food place all night.

Darren and Josie weren't initially ruled out as suspects. If they had been involved, that explained why they claimed to have no memory of that trip into the woods. But both had been thoroughly tested and interrogated, they'd passed lie detector tests and toxicology reports. They'd been poked and prodded to the point where their parents were threatening lawsuits against the police. There was no evidence whatsoever to point to the two children, no telltale blood splatter, no remains found in the woods, no connections to anyone who might be a person of interest.

Kayla believed them when they said they really couldn't recall what happened. She also knew they hadn't been involved.

She continued to dig. She read theories that Hailey had been taken by a Satanic cult that had sacrificed her to an ancient Celtic Lord of Death on Samhain. That theory even speculated that Darren and Josie were in on the plot, that their families were the Satanists. It didn't seem to matter that Darren's family had faithfully attended services at the Methodist Church every Sunday for as long as anyone could remember, or that Josie was a Buddhist and her family all had alibis on Halloween night.

Another theory suggested that a local high school kid named Randall Patrick, who liked to post about horror books and movies, had done it. Fortunately for Randall, he had an alibi. He'd been attending an all-night horror movie marathon at the Red Creek Theater with three friends. Even the girl working at the concessions stand remembered him because she'd liked his vintage *Nightmare on Elm Street* t-shirt. But news crews and crime fans had hounded Randall to the point where his family had sold their house and left Red Creek for good, moving to California.

Alien abduction was another theory. So was the one about Brigid Donnelly being a witch; that would explain why the two kids didn't remember anything—because they'd been hexed, and Hailey had been sacrificed to the Devil before her remains had been ground up and fed to pigs that it turned out Brigid Donnelly didn't even own.

Kayla was surprised that more theories didn't run with the name of the place—Ghost Woods—and suggest Hailey had been carried off by spirits.

Then there were the theories that said *she* did it, that she'd always hated her sister, that she's always been a freak who talked to demons and one had finally possessed her, that she had no alibi that night. She stopped just short of answering those posts, although it angered her to not defend herself. Of course, she *did* have an alibi—she'd been passing out candy to trick or treaters, many of whom remembered her zombie make-up.

After going over it all (again), Kayla found her thoughts circling back to Brigid Donnelly, not because of any bullshit theories about her being a witch or crazy, but because she was likely the closest person to whatever happened that night. She'd told police that something had occurred about 9:45, something that had caused her chickens to start throwing themselves against their pens in panic, but Brigid said she'd heard nothing herself. She'd even allowed police to search her yards and house. They'd uncovered only a collection of herbs drying in the barn, which Brigid grew and said she used for cooking.

Kayla had never spoken directly to Brigid. She'd seen the older woman in town a few times, shopping at Red Hook's A & P, or taking her ancient Volvo through the bank's drive-through, but they'd never met. Kayla didn't know anyone who had actually talked to Brigid, aside from the police.

According to the papers, Brigid had been born in Red Creek, in the same house she still lived in. Her family had come over from Ireland to settle in Red Creek in 1846, and lived here since. Searching through the archives of local papers and historical documents, Kayla found few mentions of them. Brigid's grandfather had once grown a prize-winning pumpkin. Brigid had a sister who'd moved to California and a brother who'd returned to Ireland. She'd been married once, but her husband had died twenty years ago, of cancer. She had a daughter who lived in Florida. Overall, the Donnellys had been quiet and unremarkable.

Kayla, though, decided she had to speak to the woman. She'd learned to trust her gut instincts, and those were telling her that Brigid knew more than she'd revealed to the police. Maybe Brigid wouldn't even speak to her, or would tell her what she'd told the police.

Kayla had nothing else, though. She had to try.

It wasn't hard to find the Donnelly place, given how many of the news articles and blogs had talked about it. It had become a frequent enough attraction for crime tourists that Brigid had put up a barbwire fence and NO TRESPASSING signs. Kayla parked at the side of the road and stepped out of her car, eyeing the surroundings. The Donnelly property was bordered on two sides by untamed meadow, now covered in gold, thigh-high grass, ready to die off at the approach of winter. A third edge ran up against Miller Road, which split the meadow; there were no other houses immediately nearby, although a half-mile distant Kayla glimpsed the newish development where the Berrys lived. The rear part of the Donnelly property backed right up against the Ghost Woods. From here the maples and elms looked dark, packed too closely together to admit light or even air, a solid organic wall of gloom.

She snapped some photos with her phone, in case they might prove useful later, and then walked up to the gate set into the barbed wire. It fronted a driveway that wound back about 200 feet to the house, an ancient two-story wood structure with turrets and dormer windows. It was in need of a new paint job—it had once been white with green and gold trim—but it was still a glorious house. Several outbuildings, including a garage, a barn, and a chicken coop, stood nearby. A well-tended vegetable patch filled the ground between the fence and the house. It all gave the impression of a resident who was orderly and self-sufficient, but offered little thought to image or the outside world.

There was a bell mounted on the fence beside the gate. Taking a deep breath, still not exactly sure what she'd say, Kayla rang it.

She waited. Nothing happened; there was no movement in the house. The Volvo was nowhere to be seen, but the garage was closed, so Kayla didn't know if it was parked there, or if Brigid was not at home. Did she even answer the bell? Was she so tired of wannabee journalists and dark tourists that she routinely ignored it? Was she standing behind the curtains in one of those upstairs turrets, squinting out?

Kayla waited a few moments. She couldn't blame the woman if she'd decided not to talk to strangers, although Kayla thought that Brigid might talk to *her*. Maybe she could find her in town, or get a message to her. She cursed herself for not writing a letter in advance, found an old receipt and a pen buried in the back of her car, wrote a small note ("Brigid—my name is Kayla Reynolds. Hailey was my sister. Please call me," with her phone number appended at the bottom). She left the note in the mailbox. It was all she could do.

As she started up her car, Kayla looked out the window at the Ghost Woods. She considered going in, looking around . . . but realized there was nothing to be gained by doing that. She remembered last year, slogging through there in the middle of the night with a flashlight, teeth chattering against the cold as she called Hailey's name over and over until she was hoarse. She'd found nothing then, and she knew she'd find nothing now. After a moment, she started the car, and made a U-turn back to home, away from the Donnelly place and the Ghost Woods.

OCTOBER 30TH, 12:30 P.M.

Just as Kayla arrived home, she got a text from Sophie: *You okay? Was worried about you last nite.*

Kayla smiled, cheered by her friend's concern. *Thanks. Sorry about that.*

Sophie: *You left the board here. I can bring it by later.*

Kayla started to respond, *No*, and then had a thought. *Thanks. Yeah, that works.*

Trying to push the thoughts of Hailey away, Kayla spent the rest of the afternoon working on a paper for her Psych class, and doing some household chores. At 6 p.m., Sophie showed up. Jess was working a long day at the restaurant (the evening manager had called in sick), so Kayla got Sophie to hang around, ordering in a pizza that they ate while guffawing at a Netflix holiday romcom.

When the movie ended (long after the pizza), Kayla asked her friend for a favor.

"Sure," Sophie said, "whatever you need."

Kayla pulled the talking-board out of the paper bag Sophie had brought it in, tossed the empty pizza carton aside, and put the board on the coffee table before them. "I want to try this again. I figure it might work with at least two of us."

As Kayla walked around and sat on the floor opposite her, Sophie eyed her friend curiously. "Are you sure? I mean, after last night . . . ?"

"I'm sure."

Kayla positioned two fingers on the planchette, waiting. Sophie hesitated, her hands hovering in mid-air. "Kayla . . . you don't actually believe this stuff, do you? I mean, this is just a game."

Lowering her fingers, resting them on the edge of the table, Kayla thought about her words for several seconds. "I heard a podcast the other day," she said, "about how belief in the paranormal always rises during traumatic events, like wars or plagues. People who have lost loved ones—who may not have even been able to see them before they died—get so desperate from grief that they'll try *anything* to reach out. That's me, Sophie. Tomorrow is the one year anniversary of Hailey's disappearance, and I'm having a harder time with that than I expected, so if this stupid board gives me a few minutes of comfort—no matter how fake it might be—I'll take it at this point."

Sophie reached across the table to clasp Kayla's hand for a few seconds before positioning her fingers atop the planchette. "Okay, so let's try it."

"I love you, Soph."

"Just put your fingers on the planchette already."

Kayla grinned, but her smile vanished the instant her fingers fell into place beside Sophie's. She took a deep breath and felt the atmosphere around her *change*, as if the energy had been sucked out of the room and returned in some other form. It sent a charge through her, starting in her midsection and arcing up to her fingers, causing them to twitch on the planchette, which didn't move.

"Hailey, are you there?"

The planchette began to slide across the polished wooden board. It landed on *YES*.

Sophie breathed out, "I'm barely touching it . . . "

"Me, too." After another inhalation, Kayla asked, "Where are you?"

H-E-R-E.

The room was noticeably colder. Kayla's eyes darted around. She saw Sophie also looking, her expression anxious. "Why can't we see you?" Kayla asked.

N-O-T-H-E-R-E.

"Here but not here," murmured Kayla, before saying, louder, "I don't understand . . . "

The planchette vibrated under their fingertips, moving swiftly now.

C-O-M-E-

Kayla lifted her fingers from the planchette, now touched only by Sophie. It continued to glide rapidly across the board.

-G-E-T-

Sophie lifted her fingers.

The planchette kept moving.

-M-E.

The motion ceased. The two women looked up, found each other's eyes. They shared a moment of wonder and fear, then Kayla said, loudly, lifting her face, "Come get you *where*? Are you in the Ghost Woods?"

The planchette was still.

Kayla returned her fingers to it, shouting out, "Goddamn it, Hailey, tell me where you are!"

Nothing.

Kayla was about to open her mouth to call out again when she felt Sophie's hand on her arm. "It's over."

Holding her breath, Kayla focused on her surroundings. Sophie was right—the charged feeling, as if the air itself was alive, was gone.

They were alone.

Looking up excitedly at her friend, Kayla said, "You felt her, right? Hailey, I mean."

Sophie was pulling back from the board, sinking into the couch cushions, clutching herself tightly. "I . . . I don't know *what* just happened . . . "

"You *do* know. We talked to Hailey."

Giving her friend a hard look, Sophie said, "I'm not so sure about that."

Trying to beat back a chill about to pass through her, Kayla asked, "What do you mean?"

"Do you know about ideomotor response?"

"No." Kayla shook her head. "No—it moved *by itself*. You saw it."

"Okay, okay, then let me ask you this: if you want to believe something really did just talk to us through this board, how can you be so sure it was Hailey?"

That stopped Kayla. She frowned, trying to relive the moment that had just passed. Had the presence she'd felt *really* been her sister? Could it have been something *else*, something impersonating Hailey?

"So, what," Kayla said, her tone angrier than she'd intended it to be, "was that Zozo? Is that what we're going for?"

Sophie abruptly rose, holding up her hands as if warding

something off. "Okay, now *I'm* the one who's freaked out. Kayla, I don't think you should touch this thing again."

Kayla didn't try to stop her as Sophie rushed from the house.

OCTOBER 31ST, 7:45 A.M.

Kayla's dreams that night were not about Hailey, but instead were filled with terrible sensations of stifling, suffocating, choked and trapped by a darkness that had mass, weight. Throughout, the only light was two green pinpoints, like shining emeralds . . .

. . . or eyes. Green eyes.

That was the image in Kayla's head when she awoke, sunlight just edging over her windowsill.

Today was October 31st—Halloween. She knew, somehow, that she had only today to solve the mystery of Hailey, only this one chance. If there was even the smallest possibility that Hailey was alive somewhere, Kayla intuited that she would have to find her and save her *today*. By November 1st, Hailey would be lost forever.

As Kayla dressed, she thought about the eyes from the dream, peering at her from the dreamworld's deep shadows. She'd seen those eyes in waking life. Grabbing her phone, she checked the hours for Halloween Beyond, saw that the store would be open in fifteen minutes. She had classes today, but wouldn't be going.

She was at Halloween Beyond when the doors were unlocked. Inside, she went from one orange apron to another until she found Maeve. The women saw her, peered at her with those same depthless green eyes. "Have you tried the talking-board yet?" A half-smile that spoke of a secret, private joke stayed fixed on her lips.

Kayla, who towered over the other woman by at least eight inches, resisted the urge to grab her by the apron straps. "I did. My sister spoke to me."

"Ahh." The ironic expression was replaced by a sympathy that Kayla knew instantly was pretense. "I'm sorry to hear about your sister."

"Why did you give me that talking-board?"

The two of them stared at each other, a battle of wills that Kayla knew she couldn't afford to lose. She let herself fall into those eyes that were the color of green leaves, of spring, of algae covering the surface of a stagnant pond, of mold growing atop something dead; she fell, but she forced herself to stay focused, to not lose herself, and when Maeve finally looked away, Kayla knew she'd won.

"There's something you should see," Maeve said, turning.

Numb, anxious even through her victory, Kayla followed through that same EMPLOYEES ONLY door, although she swore the lay-out of the hallway was different from two days ago—hadn't the break room been on the left, not the right? Had there been two restrooms? Hadn't the hallway been longer . . . or had it been shorter?

Maeve unlocked a door marked with no sign. Inside, she didn't flip a light switch. The room was already illuminated by a vague blue glow emanating from . . .

A mirror. A floor-to-ceiling mirror, oval, set in an ornately carved, old-fashioned wooden frame. Kayla found herself reflexively peering into it, wondering at the source of the light. She saw herself reflected, her body caught in that aqua shimmer . . .

No, it wasn't her. It was Hailey.

But it wasn't Hailey as she'd last seen her, a reed-thin twelve-year-old dressed in fake furs and carrying a bamboo spear like Princess Mononoke. No, this was the twenty-something Hailey she'd glimpsed in a dream—a young woman, dressed in green, her hair long, but absolutely *Hailey*.

Kayla blurted out her sister's name, and the woman in the mirror heard, looked up, saw her sister, reacted in surprise and joy and . . . desperation. She reached one slender hand out, and Kayla thought that she must surely be touching the surface of the mirror . . . if that existed on *her* side.

"You can save her," Maeve said. Kayla had forgotten the woman was still in the room with her. She reluctantly turned now to Maeve, could make out little more than her eyes in the dark room.

"How?"

"Reach out and take her hand. Pull her through."

Kayla looked back at the mirror. Hailey stood in the darkness beyond the surface, arm stretched forth, imploring, waiting. It would be so easy to step forward, take her sister's hand, pull her out of that realm into *this*, her home, her life . . .

One step forward . . . arm lifting . . .

NO.

Kayla felt it with a certainty more intense than anything she'd ever experienced. Something inside stopped her, said to her, *This is a trap.* She lowered her arm and stepped back.

From somewhere in the room, Maeve said, "You won't have this chance again."

If I'm wrong . . . but she wasn't. Nothing felt right about this. She imagined reaching those fingers and finding them *cold*, icy, strong, not yielding but pulling *her* through, to the other side . . .

"That's not Hailey."

She took another step back.

The light from the mirror faded out.

She was alone in darkness.

Panicking, she turned towards where she thought the door was. The idea of being in a lightless room with whatever Maeve was nearly made her scream. Her shaking fingers frantically moved along the wall until she found a door frame, then a knob, it twisted in her grip, the door was flung open, she staggered out into the hallway—

The door slammed behind her, and she was free.

There was no sign of Maeve, and somehow, she knew Maeve wouldn't be seen at the store again. Still shaken, her legs weak, Kayla forced herself to walk down the hallway (a normal hallway, with doors and solid concrete floor and dull fluorescent lighting) until she reached the EMPLOYEES ONLY door. She threw it open, stumbled out onto the sales floor, already busy on Halloween morning, made her way out to her car. She fell into the driver's seat and let the car's heat warm her, removing the chill that had taken her in that room before the mirror, when something had tried to lure her into a world on the other side of the mirror.

The fact that she'd won gave her little solace.

OCTOBER 31ST, 9:00 A.M.

By the time she got home again, Kayla had convinced herself that Hailey really was dead.

The Ouija board she could explain by her own desperate need to believe her sister was still alive. The moment when she and Sophie had seen the planchette move on its own . . . well, Kayla had long ago understood that there were other forces in the world, forces that no one living could possibly comprehend. She'd had glimpses of those things throughout her life, and they'd almost certainly glimpsed *back*. One of them had decided to mess with her, not so different from the internet trolls who screeched about how Kayla had killed her sister and then buried the remains "in that nice backyard garden, where things grow a little *too* well."

She didn't even know how to name what was happening to her. Was she being haunted? Had she been cursed?

The more Kayla thought about it, the angrier she got. She didn't deserve this . . . *whatever it was*. She needed information; she needed to know how to protect herself.

Her thoughts kept circling back to that name: Ghost Woods.

At home again, Kayla spent Halloween morning with her laptop, looking for information on Red Hook's most notorious area. She skipped past maps and weather forecasts and pointless chatter until she found a newspaper article with the headline "Red Creek Man Goes Missing in Ghost Woods." The article was dated 1998, and described the strange disappearance of a man named Lawrence Baird, a happily married accountant of 34 who'd walked into the Ghost Woods and simply vanished without a trace.

He'd entered the woods on Halloween.

An article from 1996 mentioned a missing woman named Martina Markov. A 1978 article about a missing six-year-old detailed a search of the Woods that had turned up one of the boy's shoes, but nothing else. There were more stories, from every decade, going back to the 1890s, when the local newspapers had started publishing.

Scanning down search results, her gaze landed on a blog post entitled "Red Creek's Ghost Woods: Two Centuries of Hauntings". She clicked on the link and found a lengthy piece, one that instantly felt grounded in fact and history, not the absurd speculation and fearmongering of so many other sites. The blog belonged to "NY Cunning Woman". It began with a detailed description of a little girl named Mabel Sanders who'd gone into the woods in 1933 and never come out. It had been Halloween night; she'd been dared by a friend, Billy Jeffreys, who'd returned alone, with no memory of what had happened to ten-year-old Mabel.

Kayla grabbed a fleecy blanket as chills ran through her.

Mabel was never found, not even a trace.

The blog's author next discussed Halloween history from

several centuries ago, when the night was celebrated in Ireland and Scotland, where the ancient Celtic belief that it was a night when the veil between worlds was its thinnest had survived. The belief in powerful fairies—once known as the *sidh*—was so strong in these areas that they were only referred to by kindly euphemisms like "our good neighbors". To do otherwise might anger them, at which point they could do anything from turn your milk sour to steal your children.

Kayla felt another chill.

She read on. What if, the author "NY Cunning Woman" theorized, there were places around the world where that veil could be parted on Halloween night? The Irish, after all, believed that certain caves were entrances to the fairies' "Otherworld", and that terrible things might issue forth from those caves on Halloween night. Barrow-mounds, ancient hillocks that were tombs, might open on October 31st, revealing fairy revels to those mortals unlucky or unwise enough to be abroad on that night; if they gave in to the temptation to join the mad festivities, they'd find themselves trapped there forever.

What if, the author theorized, there was something like that hidden in the heart of the Ghost Woods, a portal that opened on Halloween night, a borderland between worlds that might lure a child in before it shut?

There were comments on the blog post that corrected parts of it. One included a link to a 1933 newspaper article on Mabel Sanders that showed she'd actually disappeared in late April, not October. A number of responses were from people who'd gone into the Ghost Woods on various Halloween nights, only to encounter nothing spookier than two drunken college boys half-undressed and making out at the base of an old oak.

Kayla found one comment more interesting: someone who claimed to be a paranormal investigator had gone into the Ghost Woods on Halloween night, accompanied by two friends. At one point, their K-2 meters had leapt into the red just as the temperature had dropped nearly ten degrees. Although they'd seen nothing, when they later examined audio recordings they'd made, they'd captioned a clear EVP: a voice whispering, *"This is not for you."* There was a link to the recording; Kayla clicked on it, played it, heard the words just as described.

Of course, that means nothing, she thought. *It's probably one of them. They just forget they said that. Or they faked it.*

Still, the blog and the resulting comments had more information than anything else Kayla had found. Her intuition, which she'd always trusted, told her that what was happening was related to the Ghost Woods; if she could talk to the author of the blog post, maybe she could learn more. She clicked through until she found an "About" page, but it said only, "NY Cunning Woman lives in Red Creek, New York."

So, this was someone nearby; maybe even someone she already knew.

There was a "Contact" page. Not hoping for much, Kayla filled out a form, stating who she was, what had happened to her sister, and asking for help. She hit the "Submit" button, sure she'd receive no response.

She was surprised when a new message appeared in her inbox ten minutes later. She clicked on it and read: *Thank you for reaching out. I'm so sorry about what happened to your sister, but please—DO NOT GO TO THE GHOST WOODS TONIGHT. You won't find her, but you will put yourself in danger.*

Kayla re-read the message three times, considered her response, then wrote back: *I think something is messing with me, pretending to be my sister trying to reach me. I'm scared and desperate. Please help, if you can.* She knew she risked sounding crazy, but it was all she had.

Minutes went by, while Kayla continually refreshed her e-mail.

At last, the response arrived: *"Call me. Brigid."* A phone number followed.

Kayla nearly dropped her phone in shock: "NY Cunning Woman" had to be Brigid Donnelly. Who else would know so much about the history of Ghost Woods?

Fingers shaking from adrenaline, Kayla punched in the number. After two rings, a woman's voice said, "Hello, Kayla."

"Is this Brigid Donnelly?"

"Indeed, it is. And you're Kayla Reynolds."

"Yes. Thank you for talking to me. I have to ask: do you know more about what happened to my sister Hailey?"

The answer was sharp-toned. "Not on the phone. Can you come to my place so we can talk in person?"

Kayla immediately replied, "Yes," then almost as immediately regretted it. What did she really know about Brigid Donnelly? What if she really *had* been involved with Hailey's disappearance?

It was ridiculous. She was a 74-year-old woman who lived alone . . . but she also wrote a blog under the name "NY Cunning Woman." Wasn't "cunning woman" an old name for witches?

But Kayla had to accept, since there was a chance Brigid might really know more. They agreed to meet at noon. When they hung up, Kayla got a pen and a sheet of paper, and wrote a note to her mom, telling her exactly where she was going. She also texted Sophie.

Are you sure that's a good idea? Sophie wrote back.

I'm open to something better, Kayla answered.

Okay, but be REALLY careful.

Kayla promised she would.

It would take her twenty minutes to drive out to Brigid's place, so she spent the next forty pacing like a caged animal. Finally, as the time to leave arrived, she installed an audio recording app on her phone. She was almost out the door before she hesitated, then retrieved the talking-board, which she shoved into a bag.

When she arrived at Brigid's place, she pulled up, got out, and rang the bell. This time the gate rolled back, allowing Kayla to drive in. As she drove slowly down the driveway, she glanced in the rearview mirror and saw the gate rattling back into place.

She wouldn't be driving back out unless Brigid wanted her to.

She reached the house, parking in the circular dirt driveway behind the old Volvo. As she climbed out, she saw the door to the house open, and Brigid Donnelly stepped out, waiting for her.

The immediate impression she gave Kayla was one of strength. She looked her age, but she also looked like a person of determination and great will. Brigid was slender, her arms corded with muscle, her long silver mane streaming down over a simple peasant blouse worn over khakis and boots. She eyed Kayla with a mix of curiosity and warmth, and Kayla found herself thinking this woman meant her no harm . . . but she didn't completely drop her guard, either.

"Hello, Kayla. C'mon in," Brigid said, as she stepped aside and gestured into the house.

As Kayla entered, the first thing she noticed was a scent: cinnamon and lavender. The front room was spacious, framed with wide windows that allowed in a generous amount of light, decorated with furniture that was old but kept in good shape. One wall was lined with full bookcases, a mantel over the fireplace held dozens of framed photos, and Kayla had to smile as she saw a broom made of twigs tied to a long branch resting in one corner. Brigid caught the expression, returned it. "Yes, every witch has a broom."

"Are you . . . " Kayla was about to ask the obvious question when movement caught her eye. At the other side of the room, a doorway led into the kitchen, and a man was moving about there, preparing coffee. He was in his early thirties, with a long, dark brown beard, denim overalls, and a straw hat. He finished his task and turned away, moving out of Kayla's line of sight.

Brigid followed her look before asking, "Kayla . . . ?"

"Oh, sorry. I thought you lived here alone."

"I do live here alone."

"But I just . . . there was . . . " Kayla broke off.

Brigid didn't gape or scoff. Instead, she went to the fireplace and plucked a photo framed in an old, rustic wooden frame. "Is this the man you saw?" she asked.

The man in the old black-and-white photo stood in front of the barn Kayla had seen outside, holding a pitchfork; he wore overalls, a hat, and a foot-long beard. "That's him."

Brigid's expression was knowing, sympathetic. "That's my grandfather Conor. That photo was taken in 1930. He died of heart failure in 1961."

If Brigid had been anyone else, Kayla would have offered an excuse or apology. Obviously, she'd been mistaken, hadn't really seen that . . . but she guessed that she didn't have to lie to Brigid. "Do you see him around here sometimes?"

Nodding, Brigid answered, "Especially in the kitchen, which he always said was his favorite room in the house. You might also encounter my mother in her sewing room upstairs, my Aunt Lizzie in the front vegetable garden, and a very old shade in the basement I've never been able to identify, but it's good. Oh, and my childhood cat Finn occasionally saunters through the room."

Kayla felt a rush of relief, and comfort, and gratitude. She'd never spoken to someone who understood this; even though Jess accepted it, Kayla had always suspected that she didn't really believe it.

Brigid saw Kayla's reaction, replaced the photo of Conor, and stepped forward to lay a reassuring hand on Kayla's arm. "You, my dear, are far too gifted for most people to comprehend."

Speechless, Kayla allowed Brigid to lead her to an overstuffed chair, sinking into its luxurious folds that felt like a welcoming embrace. Brigid pulled a chair up closer, sat, leaned forward. "And I owe you an apology."

"You do? For what?"

"I realize now I should have reached out to you long ago, as soon as your sister was taken."

Was taken . . . most people said "disappeared", but Brigid had spoken those two words with the authority of certainty. Kayla had so many questions, but could only blurt out, "Why?"

"I've known for a while that there was someone nearby who was a powerful sensitive, but I wasn't sure who it was."

"So . . . " Kayla paused, hoping this wouldn't offend Brigid in some way, "you *are* a witch?"

Brigid's laughter was compassionate, her hand warm as she grasped Kayla's fingers. "Yes, dear . . . and so are you. You just don't know it yet."

When Kayla stared in disbelief, Brigid stopped smiling, instead looking soberly into Kayla's eyes. "Let me guess what your life has been like: as long as you can remember, you've glimpsed things that you learned early on other people didn't see. You've seen shadow figures walk across rooms, or ghosts that stood over your bed, or maybe—"

Kayla cut her off. "—not over my bed—in my closet." She'd never told anyone about the girl who was in her closet in the house they'd lived in before they'd moved to Red Creek. She was maybe seven or eight—only a few years older than Kayla had been— wearing a dress so tattered it was hard to tell what time period it was from. She was perpetually forlorn, and Kayla sensed that something terrible had happened to the girl. One day Kayla had found a Ouija board in a stack of board games in the front hallway; curious, she'd pulled it out. After reading the instructions, she took it to her bedroom, set it on the floor before the open closet, and learned that the girl's name was Amelia. A few months later, she'd heard her mom telling a friend that she thought her daughter's "imaginary friend Amelia" was "cute." After they'd moved from that house, Kayla never saw Amelia again, and hoped that she'd found another playmate . . . or had finally moved on, freed from the confines of a closet where she'd probably been trapped in *two* worlds.

"Yes," Brigid said, before continuing. "And when you told anyone else about these things that you saw, or heard, or felt, they either looked at you strangely, or told you to stop making up stories, or that it was time to give up your imaginary friend."

Kayla gasped.

Brigid's grip on her fingers tightened. "After a while, you just kept these experiences to yourself, but they didn't stop, no matter how much you tried to push them down or explain them away. What you need to understand is that you have a gift; like some people have such an extraordinary sense of taste that they can tell you every ingredient in a complex dish, or mathematicians can easily resolve complex equations the rest of us can't begin to comprehend, or a child simply knows from a young age that they weren't born in the right body, so you've been wired a little differently with *this*."

Kayla felt tears on her cheeks, but she didn't care, because this woman knew her, *saw* her . . . for the first time in her life, Kayla knew she'd been fully accepted.

Brigid rose, heading for the front door. "Let's go for a walk."

Kayla followed, silent, trying to sort out her rush of emotions. At last, she'd found someone who believed her, who might even be able to teach her . . . but this same person had been a suspect in the disappearance of her sister. Of course, so had Kayla, so that was hardly grounds for distrusting someone. She'd never met anyone else she trusted so completely. Brigid was like her house: alive, full of wild energies, of memories, of entities. Just as Kayla was thinking that, she felt something soft rub against her ankle. She didn't need to look down to know what it was. The spirits here were all good-natured and naturally good.

They walked out of the house, wound through the gardens, and followed the driveway until they came to a spot where they had an open view. Before them, the meadow, with its dry, ochre-hued brush, stretched off on the left side. To the right, the Ghost Woods formed a sharp border, almost perfectly defined. In the distance, large, new homes could just be made out. Brigid gestured at the houses. "Now one of those is where your sister Hailey was at the party, right?"

"Yes—her friend's house."

Brigid's hand shifted to the right. "See that one tree that sticks out a little from the others, with that sagging lower branch that's about to break?"

Kayla spotted it. "I see it."

"Right there is where your sister and her two friends entered the woods."

Kayla turned to stare at Brigid in shock. The older woman continued, "Yes, I lied to the police, because I saw her go into the Ghost Woods, along with the other two little ones."

"I don't understand . . . why wouldn't you have told the police about that?"

Brigid's steel-gray eyes were fixed on some unknown point. "You read my blog about the Ghost Woods, I assume, since you contacted me from that site . . . "

"I read it."

"It's all true. There are places that are gateways between our world and the Otherworld. Like Oweynagat Cave in Ireland, or the shore of Lake Acheron in Greece, where Odysseus went to call up ghosts. These places can be opened by magick, or they open on their own during certain ancient nights of power, like Samhain or Beltane. When they open, they allow the creatures of the Otherworld to come here, just as people from our side can cross over into the Otherworld . . . or be taken there against their will.

"The ancient people of Ireland knew all of this and called the creatures of the Otherworld the *sidh*. Later on, they were known as fae, or fairies. They're a capricious lot, the *sidh*; they might cross over on Samhain to wreak great havoc, they might play silly tricks, or they might kidnap an unlucky mortal they've taken a liking to. If you've ever heard the old poem about Tam Lane, you know that they can become obsessed with some humans.

"There's one of those gateways inside the Ghost Woods, Kayla. It's why my family settled here 150 years ago—so we could watch over it."

"So . . . " Kayla tried to work out the wording. " . . . you're saying Hailey was stolen by *fairies*?"

"By the *sidh,* yes. I saw the lights they carried, Hailey and her two friends. I ran after them, into the woods, but by the time I caught up Hailey was gone, the gate was closed, and the other two were spellbound, enchanted by the *sidh* to forget what they'd seen."

"Why didn't they just take all three of the kids, then?"

"I wondered that, too, but I think I know for sure now, although I've suspected for a while . . . " Brigid pulled her eyes away from the woods and looked directly into Kayla's. "It's *you* they really want."

"Me?" Kayla laughed, a small, bitter sound. "Why would they want me? I'm just . . . " She broke off, aware that she's almost said, "I'm just ordinary." She wasn't pretty like Hailey, or outgoing like Sophie, or as smart as Jess.

"You," Brigid said, taking Kayla's hands in hers, as if passing energy, power, control, "are far more gifted than you know. The *sidh* can sense talent like yours. It radiates, even if you don't know it. If you could learn to harness it, you could be a formidable foe to them—you could seal their gateways, drive them back permanently to their realm. They'd rather lure you there on your own."

"Why? If I'm so great, why not just kill me?"

"Oh, darlin', that's not how the *sidh* work. They don't *kill*; they trick, they cajole, they tempt. They might even make you a queen in their world."

Kayla staggered backward until her legs hit the porch steps, and then she sat before she fell. She was numb, dumbfounded, her mind a chaos of ideas and information. She was dimly aware at some point that she was stroking a cat, its purr vibrating against her hand. Brigid smiled as she sat beside Kayla. "I see you've met Finn. He's never come out for anyone else before."

Kayla looked down, saw there was no cat beside her. She could still hear it somewhere close by—the slight sound of the purr, claws clicking on Brigid's hardwood floors.

They sat in silence for a few moments as Kayla tried to gather her thoughts. Everything came back to Hailey, so she finally asked, "Do you think Hailey is still alive?"

Shrugging, Brigid answered, "I think so. I've dreamed about her a few times."

"So have I. For the last year I assumed she was dead, but then I started to hear her, and she came through . . . " Kayla realized she'd left the talking-board in the car. "Just a minute."

She ran over, opened the passenger door, grabbed the bag in the front seat and walked it back to Brigid. Taking the bag, Brigid peered in as Kayla explained, "Hailey came through this talking-board that the woman at the Halloween Beyond store gave me."

"Hmmm . . . " Brigid pulled the planchette out of the bag, closing her eyes, her fingers tightening around it. "Tell me about this woman."

"Her name was Maeve. Blonde, green eyes, I'm not sure how old she was . . . "

Brigid opened her eyes, returned the planchette to the bag, and said, "Maeve was *sidh*, and this talking-board is enchanted with their trickery. I wouldn't trust anything it told you."

Kayla thought about this morning with the mirror, how Maeve had vanished in the darkness, and she didn't question. "Then . . . Hailey is . . . "

"We don't know that. The only thing I can tell for sure is: if Hailey is indeed still alive in the Otherworld, she's *changed*. Things work differently over there. Nature, time, life itself, all of it has its own set of rules."

"So, do you know where the gateway is?"

Brigid rose slowly, her jaw working as she struggled with an answer. "I know you want to go after your sister, but it's too dangerous."

Anger surging through her, Kayla stood as well. "I don't care. If there's even the slightest chance of bringing Hailey home, I'll take that chance."

"You're not ready."

"Then *make* me ready. Teach me what to do."

Brigid ran an appraising look over Kayla, who involuntarily straightened up, putting on a resolute expression. "I could teach you," Brigid finally said, "but not like this. These things will take time for you to learn, and we don't have time. It's afternoon now; sundown will be here soon, and the portal will be opening. In fact, you should leave now, while it's still light. Get home, lock your doors, ignore anything you hear or see tonight."

An image came into Kayla's head then: Brigid, with an old-fashioned propane lantern in one hand, making her way through the night-dark trees. "You . . . you were going to try to save her on your own tonight!"

Brigid's eyes briefly widened in surprise, then a wry smile creased her face. "Of course, I can't hide such thoughts from the likes of you."

"Then you *have* to take me with you. You may need help, or . . . "

"Kayla." Brigid put her hands on Kayla's shoulders, holding her in a firm grip as she said, "You're too valuable in *this* world to risk."

"I'll go alone if I have to. You know I will."

After a few seconds, Brigid sighed as she released Kayla. "I *do* know. All right, girl—let's see what we can do to prepare you, then."

She led the way into the house. As Kayla followed, she couldn't shake the feeling that this just might be her last night on earth.

OCTOBER 31ST, 3:30 P.M.

It was an hour before sundown when they started preparations in earnest.

Kayla texted Jess. She didn't enjoy lying to her mother, but she thought it best to tell her that she was spending Halloween with Sophie. She didn't think the truth ("Hi, Mom—I'll be hanging out tonight with the woman who was one of the lead suspects in Hailey's disappearance") was prudent in this case.

Brigid had spent the last half-hour working in the kitchen as Kayla sat in the living room, reading an old journal. Bound in worn, flaking leather, with parchment pages covered in spidery writing, ink turning brown, the journal had belonged to a Fergus Donnelly, who had resided in Cruachan, thought to be the ancient seat of the Irish kings. Brigid had opened the journal to an entry dated "31 October 1722", leaving Kayla to read as she busied herself with preparations.

The writing was hard to make out, so even though the entry was brief it took Kayla the better part of thirty minutes to read:

31 October 1728—Samhain. I should have learned to never listen to the persuasions of Patrick O'Feeney. Patrick was born 22 years ago with a caul over his head, but in place of second sight he'd only bad luck brought on by worse decisions.

Patrick come to me as we were finishing with the harvest in the afternoon. We'd just brought in the last of the corn when he said, "Fergus, we need to celebrate." Well, everyone knew that when Paddy said "celebrate" what he meant was "drink". As we were making to leave, my mother come to me and stuck a silver needle through one side of my shirt collar. "What's that for?" I asked her. "To protect you, Fergus, on Samhain." I remembered then tales she'd told me of the fairy folk wreaking havoc on this one night, and so I left the needle in place. Mum left me to work with the other women making dollies from the corn, and Paddy and I walked the road to town. It's not a far walk . . . in the day, at least. But come night, especially Samhain night . . .

Paddy, he does like his drink. We had money in our pockets from our harvest wages, O'Shaughnessy's Tavern was full of like-minded men and a few pretty maids, and before we knew it we were drunk and it was near midnight. Pete O'Shaughnessy, he finally told us no more, that it was too cold out for him to feel fine about letting us sleep it off in his stable, so he turned us out and told us to go home. We were stumbling and loud as we left town, heading back to my farm, where Paddy could spend the night.

Well, we were maybe fifteen minutes down the road. The night was cold, so we were already huddlin' in our clothes, when we seen a light to the side ahead.

"What's that?" I asked, squinting. I was so in my cups that I could barely make sense of anything I saw.

Paddy, staggering aside me, said, "That'd be where that old barrow-hill is, now, wouldn't it?"

Indeed it was. That realization sent a mean streak of "sober" shooting through me quick as lightning. I stopped, reaching out for Paddy. "Let's go back," I says.

Just then we heard the faint strains of music comin' from the other side of that barrow, the side we couldn't see because of how the hill rose. "Someone's playin' over there," says Paddy, as he starts walking towards it.

Me, I'm clear-headed enough now that I recall what folks say about this barrow-hill on Samhain night, that a door in the side opens and you can see the fairie folk inside. They say our good neighbors play enchanted music on Samhain eve, and that any mortals who hear it are damned.

I heard it now. It spun round in my head like a busy spider wrapping up its prey. It painted pictures of dancing with the prettiest girl you ever saw, of your feet moving so perfectly that she loved you, you loved her, the night was young and the future long and you believed you'd spend it with her and—

I pulled myself out of the dream only to discover that I now stood fifty feet from an opening in the side of the barrow. Warm orange light spilled out onto the heather, a reel played by frantic fiddles wound its way through me, and I glimpsed Paddy within the barrow, on the other side of the door, his feet moving to the mad rhythms. He yelled and laughed with glee, circling a woman of beauty so extraordinary I knew instantly she wasn't mortal, but could only be fairy folk.

Paddy spun in wild circles, spied me at one turn and shouted, "Fergus, come dance!" My feet felt a pull stronger than the most ancient tides, but I defied it. I remembered, then: the silver needle Mum had placed in my collar. The music wouldn't take me as it had Paddy.

I stood transfixed, watching as Paddy danced with the good folk. The music went faster and faster, as did Paddy's feet, and at some point he stopped shouting in joy and began to frown, sweat beading his forehead. Soon he was grimacing, and the cries he uttered were anything but happy. I staggered back, trying to pull away, until my own feet lost a battle with a rock and I went down, and that was it for Fergus Donnelly and the rest of that Samhain.

When I came round again, the sun had just peeked over the horizon, the sky above me was still a deep indigo blue, and the morning was silent save for bird calls. I sat up, shivering, rubbing the back of my swollen head where my skull had met stone, and saw that the barrow-hill was once again nothing but a low grassy elevation in the midst of the flat, moss-covered landscape. I stood, and it was only then that I saw the body near me. Approaching slowly, full of dread, I saw that it was Patrick . . . or, rather, it was what was left of Patrick. When he'd gone into the barrow last night, he'd been a stout lad of fifteen stone. What lay on the ground below me had less bulk than a scarecrow, an old man's withered face, and tattered shoes that had completely worn the soles through.

Paddy had danced all night with the fairy folk, but he'd paid their price. As for me . . . my old mum's wisdom had saved me from the same fate.

Kayla closed the journal and set it aside, marveling over what she'd just read, comparing it to the diary her mother had given her, of many-times-great Aunt Hester and her Halloween party from 1890. Hester had derided the idea that her fortune-telling games could be real invocations; she and her friends had openly laughed at the Irish's servant's tales of old magic.

Tales that Kayla now believed were real. She saw now how magic had evolved down over the centuries: how it had once been as accepted as harvest, or death, or men's need to celebrate at the cost of caution. As the world changed, so did belief. Enchantments dissipated, spirits were banished, spellcraft became medicine. Yet the magic never left; it was still in the world, pushed into hidden corners, the shadowed places. Kayla saw all this as she sat in the witch's living room, feeling the presence of a phantom cat at the edge of a haunted wood.

What she couldn't see yet was her place in this secret realm. If she was as gifted as Brigid believed . . . was she here to save and protect, or did she have a darker place in this history?

The sun was just sinking below the horizon as Brigid returned from the kitchen, bearing something on a kitchen towel. As she sat opposite Kayla, she placed the towel between them. Kayla couldn't discern what the whitish, roughly pecan-sized lumps were at first.

"Did you read the journal?"

Kayla set the book down on the table beside the kitchen towel. "Yes."

"What did you think?"

"I . . . believe it."

Brigid smiled in approval. "Good. Then you'll understand when I tell you that, if we're going to do this thing tonight, our only chance is to observe certain rules."

"Tell me."

Brigid leaned forward and handed Kayla a large sewing needle, almost as long as her thumb. "That's a silver needle," she said. "Put it in your collar, behind your neck so it can't fall out or be easily removed."

Kayla did, sliding the needle through several folds of the collar of her long-sleeved blouse.

Next, Brigid picked up two of the round lumps from the towel and handed them to Kayla. "Put these in your ears when we enter the woods. We may hear the music of the *sidh* tonight; it can spellbind a mortal and pull them across the border into the Otherworld. While these won't entirely keep the sound out, they will dampen it enough to make it possible to resist . . . although it will still require some effort on your part."

The lumps had the moist, malleable feel of candles. "Are these wax?"

"Aye, but . . . well, I've added in a little something *extra*."

Kayla wanted to learn what that *something* was, but now was not the time. She wanted to learn as much as she could from Brigid, in fact. She hoped the older woman would, over time, reveal her knowledge to Kayla, become her teacher and mentor.

"Lastly," Brigid said, "you must know that you'll be subjected to sights tonight you may not understand. The *sidh* are tricksters, and they'll try their best to deceive you; you may see people you believe you know, for example."

"But what if they pretend to be Hailey?"

"Aye, they will. But . . . " Brigid abruptly leaned forward and placed a hand below Kayla's shoulder, over her heart, "you'll know *here*. Never doubt your heart. If it's really your sister, you will *know*."

Kayla was still absorbing this when Brigid rose. She put on a heavy, old flannel jacket, handed another one to Kayla, hefted a knapsack over one shoulder, and found a propane lantern near the door. "The presence of supernatural beings," she said, as she lit the lantern, which hissed in the quiet dusk, "drains electrical energy, but this will light our way."

Kayla rose, realizing they were about to leave the comfort and safety of the house and venture into the Ghost Woods. She wasn't ready.

But she followed Brigid out the door.

OCTOBER 31ST, NIGHTFALL

Kayla felt it with the first step into the Ghost Woods.

The air was charged, the temperature too low even for an October night forest. Kayla shivered, wishing she had more than Brigid's old jacket.

She also felt the comforting presence of Brigid beside her, stilling some of her rising panic. The flame in the lantern flickered, but thankfully stayed lit. It had, however, taken on a greenish tinge as they crossed the boundary into the Woods.

"I don't understand," Kayla said in hushed tones to Brigid, "I've been in here before, even on Halloween night last year when we were looking for Hailey, and it didn't feel like this."

Brigid replied, "I've never experienced this either. They're not trying to hide tonight."

They walked slowly, cautiously, feet crunching dead leaves, breath misting, senses straining.

The first voice came not very far in. "*Help meeeee . . .* " It was slight, high, a child's voice. Not Hailey's, though.

The two women stopped, listening. Ahead, something glimmered behind a tree. The voice came from that direction: "*I'm afraid . . .* "

A small figure abruptly appeared in front of the maple. A child, maybe ten, dressed in the clothing of at least a century ago, with short pants, a high-collared shirt. Kayla stared, and could see the dark brown, lined bark of the tree through him. His face was deathly pale, his eyes hollow, his mouth hanging open. When the faint voice came, the lips didn't move. *"Hellllp . . ."*

Kayla's every instinct wanted to rush forward, take the boy in her arms, comfort and guide him—but then Brigid's hand was in front of her, a warning. "He's long past help," she whispered.

Brigid led the way around the boy, giving him a wide berth, as they moved deeper into the woods. Before they'd even lost sight of him, they found another: a girl this time, no more than five or six, with cascading curls and the long, full dress of a previous century. She said nothing, simply turned dark eye sockets their way.

A teenager faded in to the right, this one dressed in the cuffed jeans and hairstyle of the 1950s. The first adult appeared to the left, and was the most fearsome figure yet: not merely thin but *skeletal*, as if every shred of fat and muscle had been drained away. Voices surrounded them, all sounding as if they were carried on a breeze from a far-distant place: *Help . . . please . . . save . . . you . . . you . . .*

The adult specter abruptly dropped its lower jaw impossibly far, creating an ebony maw, gaping, hungry. As Kayla stood looking, trembling, it shot forward, passing *through* her. She felt every molecule in her body spin crazily, as if she might suddenly, spontaneously deconstruct . . . but she stayed whole, upright.

"Are you okay, girl?" Brigid was there beside her, restoring sanity and balance.

"No . . ." Ghosts ringed them now; many of the spirits seemed mutilated or missing parts, some were simply too dim to see more than a shape. Some moaned softly, the ancient voices echoing through the tall trees.

The ghosts were moving towards them. They were trapped.

Then: an opening. Some of the ghosts moved apart from each other, creating a way out. Heart hammering, mind screaming *RUN*, Kayla started toward the narrow passage, but a hand on her arm made her spin about. It was Brigid, staring at her hard.

"We can't stay here—" Kayla blurted out.

Brigid's eyes mirrored concern, but not the terror consuming Kayla. "Work through this, girl," the older woman said. It was not a suggestion.

Kayla forced herself to examine the apparitions surrounding

them, to compare them to those she'd encountered in the past—
and she immediately realized there were differences: she didn't feel
the pressure in her chest she'd experienced before. The others—
the girl in the closet, for one—had looked real at first sight, but
these things looked like movie special effects.

"These aren't ghosts," she said.

Brigid nodded in approval. "Keep going . . . "

"They want us to run . . . " Kayla gestured at the aisle between
the specters, " . . . there."

"Yes. We'd be running deeper into the forest, not out of it."

As Kayla remembered their earlier discussions and Brigid's
blog, the final piece clicked into place. "This is a *sidh* trick."

The spirits vanished.

A voice from somewhere in the darkness said, "Well done."

Kayla knew that voice. She turned towards it, saw a figure
approaching, becoming more distinct as it neared Brigid's lantern.

It was Maeve. However, she no longer wore a cheap clerk's
uniform, but was garbed in a flowing gown of light yellow that
looked as if it had been spun from sunlight itself. It floated around
her in waves; a garland of blossoms and lush green leaves that
matched the color of her eyes crowned her long, nearly-white hair.

"You're learning quickly, Kayla," Maeve said, before glancing
at Brigid, "but with such a teacher I'd expect that."

"I'm here for my sister."

"Of course you are." Throwing a graceful hand out at the
woods, Maeve said, "And you'll find her—just follow the music."

With a laugh, Maeve leapt backwards into the night and
vanished.

They heard it now: a melody, played somewhere deep in the
heart of the Ghost Woods, a wild rhythmic jig.

Brigid placed herself in front of Kayla, said, "Remember what
I told you about fairy music."

"But we have to hear it to follow it."

Brigid answered, "Aye, we do . . . but the instant we see the
gate, the ear guards go in."

Kayla nodded, and they started forward.

With each step, the music grew louder. Kayla could make out
the instruments now: a fiddle, flute, drum. Beyond that, there was
another sound: feet on boards, pounding frantically, whoops and
laughter, hand-claps.

The music began to pull at Kayla. She felt faint, her hands twitched, her feet tripped as they fought against the spell. Kayla dug her nails into her palms, using the pain to counter the lunacy whirling around her, dragging at her—

Light appeared ahead, an orange glow. As they drew closer, they saw figures moving, dancing, backlit. Kayla closed her eyes against the sight, but the music had her, wrapping itself around her like strangling vines, thorns digging into her consciousness, she wanted so badly to let her feet find that tarantella beat and join in—

"Kayla!"

Shocked back into the present, she saw Brigid holding up her two wax plugs and then placing them firmly into her ears. When Kayla stared, almost not comprehending, Brigid grabbed her bag and yanked it. Kayla stumbled, but grasped what was happening. When she couldn't guide her fingers into the bag, Brigid did it for her, placing the wax plugs in Kayla's ears. They didn't completely shut out the music, but they dampened it enough that Kayla regained her control. She pressed on the plugs, making them as tight in her ears as possible, then nodded to Brigid. They looked into each other's eyes for a few moments, knowing Kayla's chance at rescuing her sister was at hand—along with the most dangerous moment of her life.

They neared the gate, which looked like a doorway set into a great tree trunk. Through the portal, they could see a large, comfortable room—impossibly large, since the trunk was no more than three feet in diameter. Kayla looked and thought: *I'm seeing another world.*

In that world, she could see a large, burning hearth with a cheerful fire, a table set with food and drink, musicians near the hearth playing, and at least a dozen dancers, spinning in paired circles, their feet tapping on the wooden floorboards. Although the earplugs dulled the music, Kayla still fought against the compulsion to join in. Instead, she peered at the dancers, trying to see if any of them were Hailey. None, though, were children. In fact, she recognized none of them.

Maeve stepped into the doorway, smiling in welcome, waving Kayla forward. She was so lovely, so strong, and it would be easy, so easy, to accept the invitation, to take the steps forward —no more than a dozen—to pass through that gateway into another world where she would be reunited with Hailey, and they would live with the *sidh* . . .

No. She wanted to find her way in *this* world, with those she loved. And she wanted her sister to have the same chance.

Maeve's expression changed, and Kayla knew she'd won that small battle, but this war continued. The *sidh*'s eyes glowed with crimson fury as she opened her mouth and began to sing. This was not music but a spell, to break Kayla's will. The words were in a language no human tongue had ever spoken. They rose and spiraled around each other, melodious but harsh, growing in volume, and Kayla thought she might have been deafened had it not been for Brigid's wax plugs. Kayla still felt the words within her, and she saw now: this had never been about Hailey. Brigid had guessed right: it was about *her*. The *sidh* wanted her, because something about her . . .

Her thoughts became jumbled, caught in Maeve's magic that was as old as the cosmos. It compelled her, forced her; she knew Brigid couldn't help, that she was fighting for her own survival. This was her struggle, and hers alone to win or lose.

Kayla reached deep within herself, pushing the chaotic, seductive sounds away to search, for whatever it was that both Brigid and Maeve knew she possessed . . .

And she found it.

It was within her, but not her *alone*. It was bloodlines, heritage, ancestors. She saw, with abrupt understanding, that she was part of generations of women who had stood against the forces of dark magic. They had always been there, protecting—the crones, the sorceresses, the witches. Magic had never left the world, but had been pushed back by thousands of powerful women, who guarded silently. This was why the *sidh* wanted her: because she was a threat.

With that realization, Maeve's spell was shattered. Her chant turned into a shriek of defeat, the scream of the *banshee*, the deathbringing fae woman.

The gateway began to close.

Kayla fell to the ground, exhausted, too weak to move, triumphant yet defeated—she'd failed at what she'd come here to do, even if she'd accomplished something greater. She'd kept these old ones from returning to the human world, but she'd lost Hailey forever, sealed away in that other place.

Something rushed past Kayla. It was Brigid, moving with speed that belied her years. The doorway was little more than a final, foot-wide shimmer when she leapt. A blinding flash lit the Ghost Woods.

But Kayla didn't see it.

NOVEMBER 1ST

They found Kayla a few hours later, Brigid's lantern still burning beside her. Brigid, however, was gone.

Kayla awoke as Jess and a police officer knelt over her. She said she was okay; although shaky, she got to her feet. At first, she thought she'd lost her hearing, then she remembered that she still had Brigid's earplugs in. She dug them out, thinking about the remarkable woman who had saved her.

Not Hailey, though.

Jess cried as she put an arm around her daughter, walking her out of the Ghost Woods, but there were no rebukes. She understood Kayla's inclination to come here on the anniversary of her sister's disappearance. She only wished that Kayla had told her, so they could have come together.

Kayla knew that eventually, she'd have to come up with some sort of story to explain Brigid, but she only wanted to rest. She told them all that she didn't know what had happened, and they accepted it. For now.

Kayla fell asleep as soon as Jess got her into bed, and she slept soundly for ten hours, thankful that she suffered no troubling dreams. It was the afternoon of November 1st when she awoke and dressed. Her mother was there to greet her. She'd taken a sick day to stay with her daughter, although Kayla assured her she was fine.

She wasn't, though, not completely, because she'd lost Hailey.

As Jess made them lunch, she glanced at a kitchen calendar. "Hey, that's right—it's All Saints' Day."

Kayla wondered if her mother was hoping that Hailey was with the saints now.

After they ate, Kayla took a mug of tea into the backyard. The sun cast long shadows over their garden, but the light had that particular golden shade of autumn, bringing out the colors of the dying foliage, and Kayla found it both soothing and melancholy.

She sipped the tea, marveling at its calming power. Brigid would have understood that; there was so much she could have taught Kayla, knowledge that she would now have to find on her own. Kayla tried to comprehend why Brigid had thrown herself through the closing gateway, but it made no sense. It seemed to be an empty sacrifice.

There was a slight breeze coming up from the west, scattering the dead leaves, their rustling sound combining with bird calls and the distant sounds of traffic. But there was another sound as well—a voice, slight, saying Kayla's name.

Kayla's throat tightened in fear. She wasn't ready to face something again today, not so soon, not before she was ready. Her hands shaking, she set the mug down as tea splashed out, raining down onto the earth around the backyard bench.

"Kayla . . . " The voice again, clearer this time.

Kayla rose, every nerve on edge, looking around. There was a gate in the fence that surrounded their property; beyond the gate was barren field. As Kayla watched, her fine hairs rising, the gate opened.

It opened . . . and a young woman in her twenties stepped through. She wore a long gown of green fabric that her shoulder-length brown hair flowed over, and Kayla's first thought was that she was someone who'd gotten lost coming home from a Halloween party. But she stopped when their eyes met. "Kayla?"

Kayla saw then: it was Hailey. Hailey, a dozen years older than when she'd disappeared last Halloween, but unquestionably human, living Hailey. Kayla rushed forward, gathering her sister, now impossibly older than her, in an embrace. The sisters cried together for minutes, separated to look at each other, cried and embraced again. At one point Hailey pulled back to really examine Kayla, and a combination of pleasure and perplexity crossed her features. "You look exactly the same."

"Only a year has passed here," Kayla said.

Incredulous, Hailey shook her head. "No—I kept a calendar, marked every day off. I was there with Maeve for twelve years."

"Time moves differently there."

"How do you know that?"

Kayla thought about how to answer that before saying, "There was a woman who taught me things . . . "

"The older woman who pushed me through the gateway just before it closed?"

Now it made sense. "Yes," Kayla said, feeling her eyes growing moist again.

They talked about how Hailey had been treated (well, but confined), about how she'd sometimes thought Kayla was nearby and had called out to her, about how the *sidh* had brought Hailey to the gateway last night, in case she could be of use in luring Kayla, but had spellbound her so she couldn't see through . . . until Brigid had appeared, pulled her away from her captors and shoved her through the gate. Still partly blinded and shellshocked, Hailey had staggered through the Ghost Woods, walking right past Kayla, until daylight revealed her surroundings and she'd finally made her way home.

"Home . . . " Hailey said, looking around the backyard. "I'm glad this hasn't changed."

"Now if we can just figure out how to explain you to everyone else, starting with Mom." Kayla thought then about Brigid, wondering how she would have resolved the dilemma of Hailey's aging, wondering if women like Brigid had secretly overseen these rescues and returns for centuries. Kayla knew she was one of those women, but she'd lost her mentor. She'd be starting from scratch, hoping to discover more about this past she was now a part of.

The future was hers.

NEW BLOOD

LUCY A. SNYDER

SATURDAY, OCTOBER 26ᵀᴴ, 2013

MADDIE'S MOTHER WAS gray-faced and sweating by the time they pulled in front of the grubby strip mall tucked in between two dismal, boarded-up brick fish canneries.

"Are you sure you're up for this, Mom?" Anxiety wound tight in the pit of Maddie's stomach. "We can just go home if you're not feeling well."

Her mother backed the second-hand Honda Accord into a space near the front doors of Halloween Beyond and flashed an unconvincing smile. Which quickly became a wince as she began to cough. Just like she had yesterday morning she tried to drive Maddie and her siblings to their grandmother's.

Oh God, she thought. *This is how it started with Dad.*

First, a wet cough that just wouldn't go away. Then a trip to the doctor who sent him to see *more* doctors. Her parents both pretending things would be fine and avoiding the "c" word, like it had four letters instead of six. Dad calling it "a case of crabby lungs" as if he just needed to shoo away an unwanted guest who'd arrived from the seashore. But then came the hospital for chemo and radiation. Watching his hair fall out before he shaved his head. And finally, just after Maddie's 6ᵗʰ birthday, the long, cold drive to the funeral home and cemetery.

"I think I'll just—" Her mother coughed again, her thin shoulders trembling. "—drop you off here. Gonna go back to the house for a nap." *Cough.* "Take your time in the store. Call me when you're ready." A rasping, painful-sounding inhalation.

Maddie shook her head. She didn't feel right about running around in a costume store while her mom was so sick. "I can go back with you and bring you—"

"No, honey." She breathed deeply; it sounded like the fit was passing. "You are *not* supposed to take care of me. I don't ever want you to have to do that, okay? I'm not dying, I *promise.*"

"Okay . . . " Maddie scanned the parking lot and storefronts. She didn't see any pay phones. "I don't know if the store would let me call you, though . . . "

"Oh. I forgot." Her mother dug in her huge blue purse—she and her mom both nicknamed it the TARDIS—and drew out a brand-new iPhone in a slim purple silicone case.

"Ta-dah! Happy Halloween! I figured I'd get you this instead of candy. It might rot your brain, but at least it won't rot your teeth!"

"Whoa . . . " Maddie stared at the shiny, shiny phone. She'd been pestering her mom for *years* to let her have a phone, or at least a tablet. But her mom's head was filled with dire stories of children's neurons addled by microwave radiation. Her mom had finally, grudgingly agreed to let her have a phone when she turned 16.

And it was a new iPhone! Maddie figured that her mom would get her some cheap pay-as-you-go burner at first. She'd have to prove that she was mature enough to take care of expensive technology and trustworthy enough to not abuse her digital privileges before she could get something really nice.

What had happened to change her mom's mind more than three years early?

"It's great," Maddie said. "But why . . . ?" The girl couldn't figure out how to phrase the rest of her question.

Her mother smiled again, but there was a shadow of something like fear or shame behind her eyes. "I know it's something that you've wanted for a very long time. And I know the past few months have been hard on you, what with the move and having to adjust to a new school and new people. Most of the time, you've absolutely rolled with it, and you've been great about everything. *Mostly.* So. I just wanted to show my appreciation. And I wanted you to have some fun."

Her mother held the phone out to her. "I already set it up for you and put my cell number in your contacts."

Maddie hesitantly accepted it, expecting her mom to launch into a series of conditions: no cell phone in the bedroom, no cell phone for two hours before bedtime, no texting strangers, no downloading apps without her mom's permission.

When her mom remained silent, Maddie asked, "Does . . . does it have a data plan?"

"Two gigabytes per month."

"Oh." Maddie stared down at the device, the realness of the situation finally starting to sink in. "Mom, you are the best!"

She flung herself across the seat to grab her mother in an awkward hug.

"Whoa, easy on the ribs, kiddo!" Her mother coughed again.

"Oops, sorry." She released her.

"There's just one rule regarding this phone. And it is *ironclad*. You must *not* break it, understand?"

Maddie nodded, but her stomach tightened. "What . . . what's the rule?"

"You must *not* let your stepfather see you with this phone. Like never, not at all. He's not onboard with you having a cell yet. And . . . he'll get mad that I spent so much money on it."

Maddie couldn't keep herself from grinning. Her mom had actually taken her side on something against Steve. *Finally!* But even bigger: she'd just caught her mom breaking one of her own rules.

"So, what happened to the whole 'no secrets under our roof' thing, Mom?" Maddie's cheeks hurt from smirking so widely.

Her mom gave her a sidelong look. "I guess this chick is just all out of clucks."

"Mom!" Maddie giggled, half-scandalized. That was as close to dropping an f-bomb as she'd ever heard her mother get.

"G'wan, get outta heah," her mom said, imitating an old-time mobster as she ruffled her daughter's short red hair. "Befoah I changes my mind and sends ya ta sleep wit' da fishies!"

Her mom's face suddenly paled. She covered her mouth with a shaking hand, looking profoundly horrified.

"Are you okay?" Maddie asked, confused and alarmed at her mom's sudden shift in mood. "What happened?"

Her mom nodded, seeming to regain her composure. "I'm fine. I just . . . remembered something bad. But it's fine. Go have a good time looking at costumes."

Feeling uncertain, Maddie opened her door and put one sneakered foot on the pavement before she remembered that she had a problem.

"Oh! Mom! Wait. I only have like $20 in my purse. And that's not gonna be enough to get a good costume?"

Her mother gave her a thin smile. Then reached in her purse, pulled out her black Chase credit card, and offered it to Maddie. "Here you go."

Maddie felt her eyes go wide. First, the iPhone, and now her mom was trusting her with her *credit card?* Had fairies abducted her real mother in the night and left her with a Cool Mom changeling? "Really? Seriously?"

"Yes, really. Yes, seriously." She paused, her weak smile fading. "I trust you to make good choices."

Maddie took the card and stared at it in her hand. "Are . . . are you *sure* you're not dying?"

Her mother laughed. Beneath it was the crack of heartbreak. "Don't worry about me. I'll be fine. Just go have fun, kiddo. But if you run into any problems, call me right away. My number's in your Contacts."

The girl unlocked the phone to check. "This isn't your regular number?"

"No, it's new. I splurged on a better phone for myself, too, but I'm going to hang onto my old one for a bit." She paused. "Your stepfather shouldn't know about *that,* either. Promise me you'll keep that to yourself, okay?"

"Okay. I promise I won't say anything. Love you!"

"Love you, too." She paused. "Always have, always will, even if it might not seem like it sometimes."

Elated, puzzled and worried in equal measures, Maddie put the card and phone in the pockets of her red wool peacoat, got out of the car, and shut the door. She walked a few paces toward the strip mall, turned, and gave her mother one last wave before she headed to the gaudy Halloween Beyond storefront.

FOUR MONTHS EARLIER . . .

Maddie leaned her forehead against the back row window of her stepfather's new Toyota Highlander, morosely watching the weather-beaten, navy-on-white "Welcome to Marsh Landing!" sign approach and recede. Welcome to what? There were just some bone-white dunes and shuttered, peeling bait shacks so far. Nothing she'd learned about the isolated coastal town online at the library made her feel any better about moving here. Population: 25,000. Primary exports: fish and Cosmic Cola. Total Nowheresville.

She flopped onto her side on the beige leather seat. This was probably one of those stuffy, churchy towns that forbade trick-or-treat at Halloween. Marsh Middle School was barely half the size of her old school and didn't have any Girl Scouts troops she could join. It didn't even have an orchestra. She'd only just started playing violin and already she was going to have to quit, probably.

Quitters never got anywhere in life. That's what her grandfather Ernest always used to tell her, before he had a stroke and quit living. In the months before he died, he'd argued about physics when he was alone in his room, as if the empty walls were his audience. She could play her violin in her room and pretend she had an audience, she supposed, but her bedroom walls wouldn't tell her if she dropped a note, or if her bowing was scratchy, or if her phrasing was awkward. So even if she kept going on her own, she wasn't sure she'd get anywhere anyway.

If she was honest with herself, giving up violin didn't bother her nearly as much as the idea of giving up Halloween. It was her favorite holiday, even better than Christmas, though she could never say that out loud. Her mom would say it wasn't *ladylike* to prefer Halloween over Jesus' birthday.

And Maddie's love for it wasn't just because of trick-or-treating—she could get candy any old time. Halloween was the one night when all the things she dreamed of seemed like they could actually become real. The one night when she didn't have to always be nice and demure and could be something besides a girl from a little town in a flyover state. She could be a ghost. A witch. A werewolf. Something mythical, something to be feared and respected. Running down the street in her costume, she could close her eyes in the frosty fall air and just for a moment imagine that plastic teeth and greasepaint were enamel and skin, and she could go anywhere at all on her own. What was Christmas compared to the chilly frisson of *becoming?*

"Gimme!" On the middle seat, her little half-brother Travis reached for his twin sister's teddy bear.

"Nooo!" Tiffany hugged the stuffed animal to her chest and turned away from her brother's grabby hands. "Mooom!"

"Leave your sister's toy alone." Their mother's tone was one of utter exhaustion. Was exhaustion an emotion, or the lack of it? Maddie wasn't sure. "Play with your Star Wars figures."

"Fifty," Maddie announced.

"What?" Her mother turned in her seat and squinted at her tiredly.

"That's the fiftieth time you've said those exact words on this trip."

Her mother's lips curled into a half-smile. "You counted?"

"I did." Maddie couldn't keep the satisfaction out of her voice. She was *very* good at counting. Last year she'd won a $75 gift certificate in a contest at Harmon's Grocery to guess how many jellybeans were in a big jar, and was a little sad afterward when she found out that since she won once, she couldn't compete again. She'd missed the count by 248, and was sure she could have done even better the next time.

Her stepfather, Steve, cleared his throat, obviously annoyed. "Doesn't Madame Curie have a book to read?"

Her mother shot him a dirty look but didn't say anything. Maddie felt her face grow hot. Her stepfather had started calling her "Madame Curie" after she won the school science fair with her homemade electrolysis set. And at first, it had seemed like a nice thing, as if after five years of being her stepfather he was starting to like her a little bit and to be proud of her accomplishments, like he was proud of Tiffany and Travis. After all, Marie Curie was the only person in history to win Nobel Prizes in two different sciences! So, calling her Madame Curie couldn't really be a bad thing, could it? But the way he started saying it after the first couple of times . . . it tasted like a razor blade inside a Tootsie Roll. If she said anything, he'd just accuse her of not being able to take a compliment. Of not having a sense of humor. Of being a brat.

"I *had* a book to read," she said, trying to keep her voice steady, "and I read it."

"Then you should have brought more." His tone was hard as the pavement beneath his SUV's black tires.

"I brought *four*. And I read them all." Her heart was beating so fast her vision was starting to twitch.

The twins had gone silent in the seat in front of her, like nest-bound fledglings beneath the shadow of a hawk.

"You did *not* read four books in the past six hours." He stared at her in the rearview mirror, his gaze as steady as any raptor's.

"Did, too." She grabbed her library book sale copies of *Ella Enchanted, Holes, Matilda,* and *From the Mixed-Up Files of Mrs. Basil E. Frankweiler* and held them up so he could see them. "I read them cover to cover. Ask me about them. Ask me *anything*."

She wasn't *lying*, and she knew that he hadn't enough of a clue about any of the books to even begin to question her about them. He'd made it clear he considered them to be kids' books, *girl* books, and he was a man. A man with a brand-new SUV and a fancy important job. Nothing in the books could interest him, so why bother? The idea of seeking a subject to discuss with his stepdaughter was so far from his orbit it could take him millennia to discover it.

"If you were so busy reading back there, how could you possibly know what your mother said to the twins?" There was a talon of warning in his tone: she had better stop challenging him, or else.

Or else what? she wondered bitterly. *Or else you'll take me away from everything I care about and drop me in some dumpy awful town that probably stinks of fish? Just because you got a job at some stupid soft drink company?*

Why couldn't he have gone away to work and left them where they were? Other dads did that to keep from uprooting their families. But her half-siblings weren't in school yet, so she was the only one being uprooted. Her real father had brought her mother to Greensburg so they could be closer to his father. Mom hadn't liked it there since Grandpa Ernest died. She said that seeing his old room every day made her feel sad. And Maddie wanted her mom to be happy. She *did*. But . . . ugh.

"I can count and read at the same time," she replied defiantly.

"Oh, look, they've got a Sammo's Subs," her mother exclaimed in the loud, overly cheery tone she used when she was trying to distract her stepfather.

Maddie followed her mother's point and saw the sandwich place at the end of a somewhat dingy-looking strip mall incongruously flanked by the boxy brick hulks of abandoned buildings. She didn't understand why her stepfather liked Sammo's so much. He claimed they had the best cheesesteaks, but theirs seemed to her to be made of the exact same gummy bread and greasy sliced beef all the other chains offered.

A bright orange banner at the other end of the strip caught her eye. A Halloween store! Some maybe-chain she'd never seen before called "Halloween Beyond." Perhaps living here wasn't going to be so terrible after all?

"And here's our street! Craftsman Lane!" Her mother patted her stepfather's hand on the steering wheel. "This is so exciting, isn't it, honey? Our first real house together!"

Maddie glared down at her lap, feeling a spike of irritation at her mom's comment. The old house had been real enough, but Maddie's father bought it before he died, and so it wasn't *Steve's* house. But now they could move someplace new and pretend that Maddie's real father had never even existed. It wasn't fair.

"Oh, what a lovely hibiscus!" her mother said.

Maddie looked out the window and blinked in surprise. They were on a pretty, tree-shaded neighborhood street. Teen boys were kicking a soccer ball around in a well-kept corner park that had a white gazebo and stone benches around a small pond. Were there kids her age in the neighborhood? She hadn't had a lot of friends at her old school. She and Sophie Romano were pretty tight, at least until Soph got a crush on Mike Walhgren. Maddie walked to school with Trevor Laramie for years and had thought of him as a friend until he joined Little League and decided he was too cool to hang out with girls. Sixth grade was confusing; everybody wanted to be with the boys, and nobody wanted to spend time with Maddie.

So, maybe seventh grade would be better? Maybe meeting new kids would be the one good thing about having to leave everything she knew behind?

Her stepfather slowed in front of a three-story white Victorian with a wraparound porch. "And here's our new home!"

Maddie couldn't take her eyes off the amazing porch. It had steps wide enough for pumpkins on each side, and a railing that was begging to be decorated. "That's the perfect Halloween porch!"

"Aren't you getting a little old for Halloween?" her stepfather said.

"Not yet." Maddie suddenly felt anxious. She couldn't tell from his tone if he was being serious.

"I think you are." He pulled the SUV into the driveway and parked. "I think you're getting much too old for things like Halloween and trick-or-treating."

"You said *teenagers* are too old. I'm not a teenager. Not until next April." She turned to her mother, her stomach churning. She *couldn't* be too old for Halloween. Not yet. "You said I could still trick-or-treat this year."

"Oh, honey, that's a whole four months away," her mother said. "Let's go in and see our new home!"

The house was fine. Maddie's new room got too much sun in the mornings, but as her mother pointed out, at least she wasn't running late for school anymore. Her stepfather was frequently gone on Cosmic Cola business—he bought her mother a Honda Civic so they wouldn't have to share his SUV—and frankly, his absence was a relief. Marsh Middle School was fine, too, at least as far as her classes went.

The kids were weird, though. She was used to the cliques at Wendover: orchestra kids, theatre kids, rich kids, poor kids. Good-looking kids from wealthy families who were talented at sports were at the top, and the special ed kids and the immigrant kids from poor families were at the bottom. It wasn't fair but it made sense. But at Marsh, it was mostly about whose families had been around the longest. Even the kid with crooked, discolored teeth and a limp got to sit with the popular kids at lunch because he was a real Marsh. So did the kid with the threadbare clothes. Sure, they had a hierarchy within their hierarchy, but nobody who was "new blood" got let into that club no matter how cool they were. And apparently, you could still be new blood even if your family had lived in the town for several generations . . . but meanwhile some of the other kids were considered old blood even though they'd moved to town just a few years before. The situation wasn't any fairer than at Wendover, and Maddie couldn't quite make sense of it, not entirely.

The old blood kids were actually friendlier to Maddie than they were to some of the new blood kids they'd grown up with, simply because when the teachers introduced her, they made sure to mention that her father was the new Vice President of Operations for Cosmic Cola. Maddie never would have guessed that being the daughter of an executive at the soda company would be such a big deal. It was nearly as good as being a featured soloist in the choir! She didn't make new friends, not like Sophie had been, anyway, but she always had a place to sit at lunch and kids to talk to. Best of all, nobody picked on her.

Once she realized the social advantage she had, she could never let on that she didn't even *like* Cosmic Cola. It was sickly sweet, and it had an unpleasant licorice aftertaste. And the bubbles seemed too harsh and made her sneeze. Everybody in town seemed to drink gallons of the stuff. Whenever someone offered her a bottle, she'd politely pretend to sip it and then pour it out first chance she got.

Late summer cooled to fall, and at the end of September, the janitors festooned the school in black-and-orange streamers and grinning paper Jack-o-Lanterns, black cats, and green-faced witches. Maddie was thrilled. Marsh Middle School was far more keen on Halloween than her old school was. And not only did the town have an official trick-or-treat planned from 6 pm to 8 pm on Halloween, they had special Devil's Night parties planned for older kids and teens on the days leading up to Halloween to prevent pranks and other mischief in town.

The biggest Devil's Night party—or at least the most *important* party as far as her classmates were concerned—was the Cosmic Cola Party at Marsh Mansion up on the cliff above the ocean. None of the Marsh family lived there anymore. Old Jeremiah Marsh had donated it to the soda company for charity events and executive retreats. They'd ride in a chartered bus up the winding road to the mansion, and at the party, they'd dance and drink Cosmic Cola and eat pizza and play games. All that, on the face of it, didn't seem so impressive to Maddie, but the old blood kids all talked about how their parents had said that the company was bringing in a super-secret special guest to play at the party. Some said it might be Miley Cyrus . . . others claimed it was Justin Bieber or even One Direction.

Maddie's mother said she was far too young to go to a rock concert, so to think that she might be able to see someone like Justin Bieber . . . that was *most* impressive. And even better, because the party ran so late, all the kids who attended would be excused from school the next day.

The catch was that only thirty kids could attend the party. They'd be chosen in a special lottery a week before Halloween. Everyone got one ticket, but students could earn extra tickets by making As, volunteering to help out around the school, etc.

By October 7th, she'd earned seven lottery tickets thanks to her good grades in math, English and history and a couple afternoons picking up trash. Seven was more than most kids, but she guessed that there were probably 900 tickets total for the 300 kids in the school, which meant that her efforts had earned her only a fraction of a percent of a chance.

And then she had a worrisome thought.

"Papa, I was wondering about something," she said that night at dinner. Her mother and stepfather preferred that she called him Papa, rather than Steve or Mr. Gibbs. Calling him that almost didn't seem unnatural anymore.

"Yes?" He took a bite of meatloaf. "What is it?"

"The Cosmic Cola party . . . you work for the company. I won't be excluded from the lottery, will I?"

"No, not at all," he replied cheerfully. "You've got as much of a chance as any other kid. Better, I expect, since you got all those extra tickets."

Her mother suddenly looked anxious. "You shouldn't get your hopes up, honey. So few kids get picked. But don't worry. There are plenty of other parties that evening. There'll be a sock hop party at DiLouie's Pizza; that sounds like fun, don't you think?"

Maddie shrugged and ate her mashed potatoes. No one cool was going to show up at a sock hop. And the pizza parlor wouldn't have Miley Cyrus except on the jukebox.

Her stepfather fixed his sharpest gaze on her mother. "But if she *is* chosen, it's an honor to go."

He turned back to Maddie and smiled. "Cosmic Cola is putting a lot of effort and money into this party for you kids. If you're chosen, you'll be representing our whole family, so you need to be on your best behavior. Can I count on you?"

His words made Maddie feel uneasy. How could a party for a bunch of middle schoolers really be such a big deal? But she knew what he wanted to hear. "Yes, sir. You can count on me."

She looked at her mother. Her face had gone white, and she was staring down at her half-eaten plate. Her mother's expression was carefully blank, but her eyes shimmered as if she were holding back tears. It was then that Maddie realized that her mother was not happy, and something was happening here that Maddie didn't understand. She wanted to go around the table to give her mother a hug, but she knew that would break some unwritten, unspoken rule; her mother would be embarrassed, and her stepfather would be angry, but neither adult would tell her what was wrong. Maddie felt as though she were a boat adrift far from shore beneath storm-gathering skies.

NEW BLOOD

On Thursday, October 24th—exactly a week before Halloween—the school held the drawing for the Cosmic Cola party in the gymnasium. Teachers and staff herded all the kids into the gym and onto bleachers just after lunch. At first, the whole thing was wildly exciting. But as the tenth, then the fifteenth names were called, Maddie started to feel a bit antsy and bored. Worse, the hard wooden bench was making her tailbone ache.

For the sixteenth time, the school's portly vice principal reached into the clear plastic raffle tumbler full of names on folded white notecards. He picked one out and opened it with a theatrical flourish.

"Maddie Flynn," he announced into his microphone.

Maddie sat in shock at hearing her name called. The girl beside her started shrieking in excitement and shaking her shoulder, and soon Maddie was whooping and high-fiving the other kids near her who'd been chosen for the party, too.

After the school assembly was over, Maddie had study hall, and her excitement faded into curiosity. She and 21 other new blood kids and eight old blood kids had been picked. Why had so few of the old blood kids been chosen? The kid with the limp and the crooked, discolored teeth was one of them. She still wasn't sure what his name was. But, she reasoned, the old blood kids hadn't tried very hard. They hadn't been the ones volunteering for chores to earn extra tickets. They hadn't studied late trying to earn straight As. They weren't the ones who had to prove they belonged in Marsh Landing.

When she got home and told her parents the news, her stepfather seemed pleased, and her mother smiled and congratulated her. But Maddie could see something like panic in her eyes, and she didn't understand why.

Very early the next morning, when it was still entirely dark out, Maddie groggily awoke to her mother gently but insistently shaking her shoulder.

"Shh!" Her mother warned, as the girl mumbled a complaint. "Get dressed, and get your things. No time to waste."

"What's going on?" Maddie rubbed her eyes.

"We're going to your grandmother's," she replied lightly.

"But . . . it's Friday. I have school?"

"Don't worry about school. It's a surprise for her birthday."

"I thought her birthday is in January?"

"It's going to be an extra-surprising surprise."

Underneath the lightness of her words, her mother sounded so grim and frightened that Maddie didn't question her further. So, she gathered her books and some changes of clothes and shoved everything in her purple backpack.

Her mother worked a sheer miracle in the next few minutes by getting Travis and Tiffany dressed and downstairs with only a few sleepy whines.

"Where's Papa?" Maddie asked, confused.

"He's still asleep. Be quiet so you don't wake him."

"Is . . . is he not coming with us?"

"He is not." Her mother's tone was firm, final.

Maddie was frankly thrilled to not have to spend most of the day in the car with her stepfather . . . but this abrupt early-morning departure alarmed her. Were they really going to her grandmother's? Was her mom getting a divorce? Could her mom be in trouble with the cops or government or something? An image rose in her mind of her stepfather lying blue-faced in bed, dead from being smothered with a pillow. Maddie silently vowed to be a good alibi. Meanwhile, her mother's expression and body language told her that this was not the time to ask questions.

The trouble began soon after the Honda's headlights hit the "Now Leaving Marsh Landing . . . Come Back Soon!" sign.

Her mother suddenly made a choking noise, and her hand went to her throat.

"Mom, are you ok?" Maddie asked from the front passenger seat.

"Yes, I —"

Then her mom started coughing, gasping for air. Her face turned red as if invisible hands were strangling her. This reminded Maddie a little of a classmate who had an asthma attack, but this seemed so much more sudden, more violent. She didn't know what to do.

NEW BLOOD

While Maddie sat frozen and mute in fear, her mom pulled over onto a patch of gravel shoulder illuminated by a tall yellow roadway light. She clumsily parked, threw open the driver's door, and started to cough hard. She retched wetly onto the pavement.

"Mom!" Maddie's body finally responded to her brain again. She unbuckled her seat belt and opened her own door, intending to run around the car to hold her mom's hair or try to do CPR or something—

—She screamed as a man's hand closed around her upper arm and pulled her from the car.

"Calm down, kid," the man said sharply as he hauled her to her feet.

His voice was familiar. He sounded like her stepfather's executive assistant, who she'd spoken to a few times when he called the house. She blinked at his dark face silhouetted by the buzzing yellow lamp.

"M-Mr. Creek?" she stammered. She looked behind her mother's car to see where he'd come from. Her stepfather's SUV was idling a few yards behind. "Is Steve—I mean, Papa here?"

"Your father phoned me and asked me to pick you kids up." His eyes flicked impassively to her mother, who was still coughing horribly. Just like her father had when he started to get sick.

"He'd have come himself, but he's too groggy to drive right now." Mr. Creek scowled at her mother's trembling back, and his hand tightened on Maddie's arm.

"What about my mom?" She tried to twist free of his grip, but couldn't. "She's sick, you need to take her to the hosp—"

"She'll be fine once she goes back home." His voice was loud. Was he making sure her mother could hear him over her coughing? "She should have known better."

"W-What's wrong with her?" Maddie stared at Mr. Creek.

"Nothing that won't be cured by attending to her wifely duties," he muttered. "Don't worry about her, kid. She'll be fine. Help your brother and sister get into your father's car. I'm taking you back to his house."

"But—"

"No 'buts', kid. Move it." His voice turned sarcastic. "Mrs. Steven Gibbs can drive herself back where she belongs."

Her stepfather was sitting on the living room couch in his blue bathrobe when Mr. Creek ushered her and her sleepily whining siblings through the front door. He was sipping a mug of coffee. His hair was mussed, and his eyes glassy, as though he'd gotten drunk.

"Thanks, Al," he slurred.

"Absolutely, Mr. Gibbs. I expect your wife will be home shortly."

Her stepfather grunted, frowning, and set his mug down on the glass-topped coffee table. His eyes flicked over to Maddie, and his scowl deepened.

"You kids go back to bed," he said. "Get some more sleep before school."

"We're still going to school today?" Maddie asked, hoping against all her experience that he'd relent.

"Absolutely." He stood and stumbled over to loom above her. "And you won't mention what just happened to anyone, hear me?"

"Yes, sir."

Her mom woke her up shortly after Maddie snoozed her alarm and ushered her downstairs for pancakes and bacon with her siblings at the kitchen table. Mrs. Gibbs shushed them when they started to ask any kind of questions at all.

Her mother's morning cheer and chatter was so usual, so normal that Maddie was almost convinced that she'd simply dreamed the car ride.

Except her mother's pallor, the bruise-colored circles under her eyes, and her occasional wet cough betrayed the gaslit lie.

The next day, Maddie found herself standing on the sidewalk in front of Halloween Beyond. The window displays were filled with spooky animatronics of witches and zombies, along with dummies dressed in all kinds of costumes and masks. Some were posed to look like they were flinching away from the animatronic monsters. Black plastic curtains festooned with fake cobwebs hung behind them, blocking window shoppers' views into the store. The glass door was similarly covered in black plastic, and upon it hung a fluorescent green sign with black-edged blood red letters in a deranged, jagged font: HALLOWEEN BEYOND. ENTER IF YOU DARE!

The occult trappings simultaneously unnerved and thrilled Maddie. If the costumes inside were even half as good as the ones in the window display, she was certain to find an excellent one. So she pushed inside, and rocked back on her heels at the sudden blasts of sights, smells, and sounds.

The place was much bigger than she'd guessed it could possibly be, and it was filled with more animatronic monsters and rows upon rows of costumes, masks, candy, snacks, Halloween décor, candles, toys . . . anything anyone could possibly want for Halloween seemed to be packed into the place. This store was far, far cooler than any of the other Halloween chain stores she'd been to. She couldn't believe she'd never even heard of it before, and it straight-up blew her mind that it was in a town like Marsh Landing.

The sheer number of choices was dizzying. So, for a long while, Maddie simply wandered through the rows, gazing at everything, touching, admiring, her face aching because she was grinning so widely.

"You look a bit lost . . . may I help you?" asked a woman a few feet behind her.

Maddie turned. Before her was the most lovely, striking, positively ethereal lady she'd ever seen in her life. Her skin was pale, almost pearly-looking, and her long silvery blonde hair was pulled back in a complicated braid. Her eyes were the deep, shimmering green of secret rivers and hidden forest glens.

Seeing her in this town was like stumbling upon a rare orchid growing in the middle of a desolate salt flat. Maddie looked all around, searching for camera lenses or some sign that she'd actually stumbled onto the set of a Hollywood movie. Because this lady *had* to be an actress or a model or a queen from some foreign land or *someone* important. She couldn't be a store clerk, even though she was wearing an orange Halloween Beyond apron. Her neon green nametag said her name was Maeve.

She looked at Maddie expectantly, her eyebrows raised, waiting for the girl's reply.

"Oh. I . . . uh . . . I came to get a costume?"

"Wonderful! Is it for trick-or-treating, or is it for a special occasion?" The lady's accent was a bit odd. She certainly wasn't one of the locals. Maybe she was from Scotland? Or Ireland?

"It's for the Cosmic Cola party . . . I got picked in the lottery."

"Well! That certainly is a special occasion. Have you thought about what you'd like to wear?"

Maddie considered. "A little. I liked being a witch last year, but I don't want to do the same thing, you know? I was sort of thinking I could be a werewolf this year . . . I saw a cool mask on a dummy in the front windows."

"Not a bad choice. But, in my professional opinion, werewolves are just a bit played out. Not as played out as zombies, but still a bit ordinary," Maeve said. "Are you open to suggestions?"

The girl shrugged. "Sure."

"Why don't you go as a pirate queen?"

Maddie blinked. "A pirate queen?"

"They probably didn't tell you this in school, but a lot of women were very fierce pirates back in the day. For instance, Jacquotte Delahaye was a Caribbean pirate in the 1600s. They called her 'Back from the Dead Red' after she faked her own death to escape the British Navy. She became a pirate after her father died and, eventually, she became a master swordswoman and commanded a fleet of hundreds of pirates. She ruled over her own island. I think ruling your own island makes you a proper queen, don't you think?"

"Whoa," Maddie said. Already in her mind she was swashbuckling on a beach, protecting a loot-laden chest from scowling English redcoats in pompous white wigs. "Yeah, for sure!"

Maeve smiled and beckoned her down the aisle. "Then I have just the costume for you. Follow me."

Barely able to contain her glee, Maddie skipped across the pavement to her mom's car, put her bags on the back seat, and bounced into the front passenger seat.

"Well, you're in a good mood," her mom said. "I take it that costume shopping went well?"

"Oh my gosh, Mom, Halloween Beyond is so cool! And this lady who works for the store, Maeve? She found me the coolest pirate costume *ever!* It's got this pretty blue silk scarf, a white blouse with laces and embroidery, a real leather vest with brass buttons, tall leather boots . . . and the wig! Oh my gosh, it's so pretty. It looks like something from a fancy salon! And the pirate cutlass. It's just plastic, but it looks like the real thing. And Maeve even got me a flask to keep in my vest so I can bring lemonade. That way, I don't have to drink any of that nasty Cosmic Cola."

Her mother laugh-snorted as she pulled out of her parking spot. "A flask, eh? I wouldn't have expected a Halloween store would carry those."

"They have *everything*! Maeve even found me this cool black cat waterproof phone case." Maddie pulled her phone out of her pocket to show her mom.

"Wow, kiddo, you scored quite the haul!"

"Maeve warned me to not let people see the flask, or they might think I was drinking something I shouldn't and get in trouble."

"Maeve sounds like a smart lady. You probably shouldn't let your stepfather see the flask, either."

"Gotcha." Maddie paused. "You look like you're feeling better?"

Her mom smiled. "I am. I got a lovely nap while you were shopping, and I have a lot more energy than I did."

"Do you think you have enough energy to carve pumpkins with me this evening?"

"Absolutely!"

On Devil's Night, Maddie's stepfather had some kind of meeting he had to go to, so he wasn't around when her mother helped her get dressed in the rented pirate costume for the party.

"There." Her mother adjusted the red wig, which was much heavier than Maddie had expected, as were the lemonade-filled flask in the left inside pocket of her vest and her iPhone in its waterproof case in the right. Strangely, the plastic sword hanging against her left hip seemed heaviest of all. "Perfect. Turn around and take a look."

Maddie did. The wig and her mother's makeup job to give her a proper Caribbean tan made her look much older, but more importantly, she looked like a real pirate!

Maddie threw her arms around her mother's neck. "This is great! Thank you sooo much!"

Trembling, her mother returned the hug, rubbing Maddie's back in gentle circles. "It's your last Halloween, and you're going to a very important party, so I wanted you to feel proud of your costume."

Maddie hugged her mother more tightly. "You're the best."

Her mother began to cry and shake.

Maddie pulled back and gazed at her mother, worried. "What's the matter, Mom?"

"Nothing, nothing." Her mother quickly wiped her red eyes and smiled widely. Unconvincingly. "I . . . you're just growing up so quickly. It makes me sad sometimes."

Her mother started stowing the makeup back in her kit. "You know how to use the map app on your phone to get around, right?"

Maddie squinted at her. Did her mom think she was stupid or something? "Of *course* I do."

"Make sure you keep your phone with you. Keep it on airplane mode in your pocket and don't let the chaperones see it; they're probably going to confiscate everyone's devices to keep people from taking photos. You need to be able to figure out where you are, just in case they take you out someplace and you get separated from the rest of the kids. It's easy to get lost in an unfamiliar town, you know?"

Maddie didn't, but she nodded anyway.

"Marsh Mansion is due southeast of here. If you had to get back here on your own, go north on Oceanside Highway and follow it to 6th Street, go left, and then take a left on Craftsman Lane. And you'll find us."

That sounded like a whole lot of walking. "If I got lost, couldn't I just call you to pick me up?"

"Oh, of course, but please text me on my new number instead of calling," her mother replied quickly. "Your stepfather's concerned about prank callers, and he's planning to leave the landline off the hook. And I'm planning to keep my phone on silent once it gets late. He hasn't been sleeping well and you know what a terrible mood he gets in when something wakes him suddenly."

Maddie did. "Okay, I'll text you if something happens."

"But nothing will! This is all just for contingency's sake. I'm sure you'll have a wonderful time."

"Okay."

Her mom set the makeup kit aside, turned to Maddie, and hugged her tightly. "You know I love you, right?"

"Of course," Maddie mumbled into her mom's shoulder.

"I love you bunches and bunches. I know that, sometimes, I do things that don't seem fair, and I'm sorry about that. I just can't change how some things are." She paused, her body seeming to hitch with a stifled sob. "Steve and I have to worry about what's best for the twins, and . . . well, let's get you to the party."

By the time Maddie's mother dropped her off at the school stadium parking lot, the 29 other kids were clustered under a tall light, giggling and horsing around as they waited for the Cosmic Cola chartered bus to pick them up. Fifteen boys, and fifteen girls. Seven of the girls were dressed up as different kinds of witches; three were fairy princesses, three were black cats, and one was dressed as Katniss Everdeen. Amongst the boys, there was a Han Solo, a Thor, a cop, two Captain Americas, a Batman, a Superman, a soldier, several zombies, a masked slasher . . . and a pirate captain, who she was dismayed to realize was the old blood kid with the limp and crooked teeth. It made her feel weird that they'd chosen similar costumes. She felt her cheeks heat with embarrassment when he looked up at her and grinned and waved.

The Cosmic Cola bus rolled up, and a pretty woman in a mini-skirted, black-tie magician's costume stepped out onto the pavement holding a black satin bag that might have actually been a pillowcase. A couple of the boys whispered she was dressed like a character named Zatanna from the comics, and once again Maddie was annoyed that her parents had forbidden comic books, because she hated knowing less than the other kids.

"Hey, kids!" Zatanna beamed at them all, then reached into the bus and pulled out a red milk crate, which she set open side up on the pavement to the left of the bus door. "Are you ready for the party?"

The crowd exploded in "Yeah!" and "Woo!"

"Excellent!" She stepped forward and opened the black satin bag. "Everyone line up in front of me, and take a Ziplock out of this bag. Just one person at a time. Your Ziplock will have a Sharpie marker inside. I want you to write your name on the outside of the bag, and seal your phone inside." She pointed at the crate. "Then put your phones in here before you get on the bus."

The cheers faded into a stunned smattering of "Whaaat?" and "Aw, man!"

"I'm sorry it has to be this way, but we have a very special guest tonight and they have a strict policy of absolutely no photos. We know you're good kids, but the temptation might be too great when you see who's there. So, we have to take them before you can go to the party. I *promise* we'll take great care of your phones."

Zatanna crossed her heart with her index finger.

Still grumbling, the kids all lined up as she'd asked. Maddie got in line, too, her heart pounding partly from her excitement at wondering who the guest was . . . but partly from anxiety over her phone. It was tucked out of sight in her vest, but Maddie knew she was a terrible liar. *All* the other kids had phones. It was expected. How was she going to bluff her way out of it?

So she shuffled along, wracking her brain, growing closer and closer to the embarrassment of being found out.

And suddenly she was there in front of Zatanna, who held the satin bag of bags out to her.

"I, uh . . . " she stammered.

"Maddie doesn't have a phone," a boy announced a few feet behind her.

She turned, and saw to her dismay that her rescuer was the strange kid in the pirate captain costume. He waved at her, grinning.

"Her mom thinks phones cause brain cancer and won't let her have one," he added.

The other kids laughed, and Maddie felt her cheeks grow hot.

Zatanna smiled at her pityingly. "Go find a seat."

Maddie hurried onto the bus and plopped down on a plush red velvet window seat near the middle . . . and her heart dropped when the weird kid sat down beside her a few seconds later.

"Hey." He extended his hand. "My name's Hubert. My mom won't let me have a phone, either. But it's because I'm clumsy and she thinks I'd break it."

She awkwardly took his hand and shook it. "I'm Maddie."

"Yes, I know. Your father's the new executive. He must be so proud that you got chosen."

Maddie squirmed in her seat. Hubert was looking at her so intently, and . . . it was all just so weird. "Yeah, I mean, I guess."

"*My* father's *super* proud." Hubert gave her a snaggle-toothed smile. "He was always so disappointed that I was born with my legs messed up, and the doctors couldn't really fix them, but now I get to do something really good for the whole family tonight."

"Why is this party such a big deal?"

"Well, it's the thirty-year . . . " He paused, wincing a little, seeming to realize that maybe he'd said something he shouldn't. "Um. It's just going to be something special. You'll see."

Zatanna went up and down the aisle with a narrow serving cart laden with apple cider donuts, popcorn balls, bags of chips, frosted Halloween cookies, and of course, cans of Cosmic Cola.

"They'll have pizza at the party, too." Hubert grabbed double-fistfuls of donuts. "You want something?"

"No, thank you. I think I'll save room for pizza." Feeling unsettled, Maddie turned away to watch the Marsh Landing Lighthouse and the rest of the dark landscape pass outside the bus windows.

They reached Marsh Mansion just before 9 pm. It was a huge old place, built on a low cliff above the ocean, all covered in Victorian gingerbread and wrought iron balconies and railings.

Zatanna and the bus driver—a gruff, heavyset man who'd been silent the entire trip—ushered them all off the bus and into the mansion's vaulted foyer.

"Last year, we had the party in the second-floor ballroom, but there was a leak and some of the ceiling came down last week," Zatanna said brightly. "So this year, the party is in the grotto."

She opened up a pair of double doors at the side of the foyer that revealed wide stone steps with a wrought iron wall railing that coiled downward. The bass line of Michael Jackson's "Thriller" boomed faintly from below. "Everybody, follow me!"

The kids all jostled down the stairs. Maddie gripped the iron railing, partly to avoid getting knocked over, but partly to still her nerves, which had been jangling ever since Hubert's comment. She felt bad for judging the boy on his looks, and after all, he had been very nice to her. But it wasn't just his appearance that made her recoil, and her instincts told her that anything he liked, she should be wary of.

That's silly, she told herself. *Everyone says this party was a huge honor. Everyone.* Her stepfather, her mother, the vice principal, the other kids. It wasn't possible that everyone could be wrong.

The railing was very cold, and slick from condensation. The air grew colder and damper and the music got louder as they went down, down at least three stories into the earth. She was glad for the cover of her vest. The widely spiraling stairs were at first lit with electric lights, but those changed to guttering, Medieval-looking torches in iron sconces.

"Mind the open flames." Zatanna called up over the music. "Don't get burned!"

Just as the music switched to "This Is Halloween," the stairs opened up into a big natural cave whose walls were strung with white-and-orange string lights. Along the left side was a big buffet line with a half-dozen pizzas from DiLouie's in white cardboard boxes and a few steel banquet serving bins atop flickering Sterno cans.

At the end of the long table beyond the food were plastic tubs of Halloween special edition Cosmic Colas on ice. The orange label cola was supposedly flavored with pumpkin spice, and the green one like caramel apples. Maddie hadn't seen either variety for sale anywhere, and her stepfather never brought it home, which made her suspect it didn't taste any better than the other flavors. They had diet versions, but there wasn't even any water. Maddie was glad she brought her flask.

On the right side of the cave were some big heavy steel barn doors which had either corroded or were painted a rust brown. A bit of water puddled beneath them, and Maddie wondered where they led.

The side of the cave directly opposite the stairs held a raised stage with a few big speakers and some sound equipment but no instruments. A DJ in a black turtleneck and jeans and a pair of huge headphones sat at a laptop with a couple of turntables beside the stage. He gave her a little wave when he noticed her staring at him, and that made her flush with embarrassment and look away. And when she looked away, she noticed four other men—Chaperones? Security guards?—standing quietly in alcoves carved into the limestone walls. They were also dressed in black, and at first glance she thought they were statues or decorative dummies, but then one scratched his nose.

"Dig in, kids!" Zatanna shouted over the booming music. "Our very special musical guest will be out in a little while!"

The seventh graders swarmed to the food line, chattering and pogoing with excitement as they flopped pizza onto paper plates with greasy fingers. The other kids had gotten increasingly rambunctious as they'd drunk more soda and eaten more sweets, and the louder they all got, the more Maddie lost her appetite and wished she could be someplace that wasn't so noisy. And that frustrated her. She was finally someplace cool with the cool kids; why couldn't she enjoy it? Why couldn't she just join in like everybody else?

Was this what getting old was like? To feel isolated in the middle of a huge crowd and want to be someplace quiet? To feel oppressed rather than privileged to be in the middle of something everybody said was cool?

The DJ cued up "I Put a Spell on You" from *Hocus Pocus* and a bunch of the kids started dancing, Cosmic Cola cans sloshing in their hands.

"You should get some pizza!" Hubert yelled at her elbow.

She turned toward him, startled. His eyes were glassy, and he had an enormous grin on his sweaty, flushed face. He gripped what had to be his third or fourth Cosmic Cola of the evening.

"I will," she yelled back. "In a minute or two,"

"Okay," he replied. "I'm not trying to boss you around. It's just you should enjoy yourself. You earned it!"

I should, she thought. *I should stop being a stick in the mud and get some pizza, at least.*

Just as she made her way to the back of the buffet line, she saw a group of men and women in strange, hooded robes come down the stairs in single file. Startled kids stopped dancing and let them pass as they made their way to the stage. When the last hooded figure—the 13th—had emerged from the stairway, two of the silent men in black suits pulled an iron gate Maddie hadn't noticed over the entry to the stairs and chained it shut. The girl's stomach dropped, and she lost any and all interest in pizza.

The DJ stopped the music and turned on the stage lights. Zatanna stepped up and approached the microphone.

"And here's our special musical guests tonight, direct from Innsmouth," she announced. "The Esoteric Order of Dagon Choir! Let's all give them a hand!"

Some of the new blood kids started golf-clapping uncertainly, but Hubert and the other old blood kids started cheering and whistling and stomping their feet and chanting like they were at a football game: *"FAA-ther DAA-gon! FAA-ther DAA-gon!"*

Maddie blinked, feeling profoundly confused and unsettled. This didn't make any sense. Was Father Dagon the lead singer? Or was it the name of a song? What was going on here?

Zatanna hopped offstage. The leader of the group pushed his hood back and stepped regally to the microphone. The old, thin, white-bearded man scanned the crowd of kids. He wore a strange golden crown that was all high, asymmetrical spires in front with some coralline flourishes around the headband. It looked like something someone found at the bottom of the sea and something she'd expect to see floating in outer space.

"You are the Chosen," he intoned into the microphone. "You are the Promised. You are the Honored. Tonight, you ascend as you descend, and the gift of your lives ensures that Father Dagon smiles kindly upon your families and communities for the next generation. Those of you whose families are outsiders, rejoice! From this night forward, your sacrifice ensures that your bloodlines flow with ours. Your kin will be joined with the host, and you will all be profoundly blessed."

Maddie felt her heart flutter in her chest, and she took a step back, bumping into Hubert. The gift of their lives? *Sacrifice?*

"Father Dagon, take me first!" Hubert screamed behind her.

Maddie frantically looked around for some other exit, or a place to hide, but there was none. Just the heavy metal barn doors that led someplace dark and watery, and the chained gate to the stairs.

The man with the crown took a deep breath, as did the twelve choir members behind him, and they began to sing. It was loud, like opera, but there was no melody and the voices of the chorus ground against each other like glass in disharmony. Maddie's whole body broke out in goosebumps, her heart pounded in her chest, and she plugged her fingers in her ears. But there was no getting away from this strange, horrible, atonal music, no way to keep it from pounding into her skull like hurricane waves smashing against the beach, no way to keep from feeling like someone was reaching inside her skull and twisting her brains until up was down and down was up, and it was all so terrible that she just wanted to laugh and laugh and never stop . . .

And the other children around her were laughing, laughing 'til they shrieked, laughing 'til they vomited up pizza and sweets and Cosmic Cola. The still-sane part of Maddie's mind noticed that Zatanna and the men had gotten out hard-shelled earmuffs like her stepfather wore when he went to the gun range. And they just stood there on the margins, wearing their ear protection, impassively watching and waiting . . . for what?

Hubert finished puking behind her and gasped, "It's happening! It's happening! Praise Father Dagon, I am Becoming!"

She turned. The boy's whole head was swelling up like a grotesque balloon, his eyes bulging, his mouth widening impossibly. His back and shoulders hunched spasmodically, and she heard the crack of breaking bone. He yawned, making a terrible retching sound, and Maddie watched in horror as his crooked white incisors, bicuspids and molars popped bloodily from his jaw, jumping free like popcorn kernels, only to be followed by the sharp grey irregular jags of brand-new teeth erupting through his raw gums, teeth like a shark's or a barracuda's. His eyes had bulged so much she was sure they'd pop right out of his head, the whites turning black, his blue irises turning a mottled golden like a frog's.

His skin split over his swollen flesh, and he started furiously scratching himself with newly-clawed paws, tearing his clothing and pale skin away to reveal mottled, moist scales beneath. He threw the last rags of his captain's costume aside and crouched naked on muscular frog's legs, croaking hoarsely at her.

The awful sight of Hubert's transformation sent adrenaline surging through Maddie's blood, and that broke the spell of the eldritch choir. She stepped away from the hopping abomination that Hubert had become and looked all around her, again seeking escape when she knew there was none. All the other kids were turning into monstrous fish-frogs. Everybody changing into something mythical and terrifying. Everyone but her.

The sane, calm part of her mind made note that while the dark part of her mind had long dreamed of being able to become something feared and respected, something that could send all the kids who'd ever bullied her and all the adults who'd ever belittled her screaming for the safety of locked doors . . . she most certainly did not want to become one of these god-awful things. They *stank*. Sweet lord, they stank like fish and vomit and blood. And one look in their bulging eyes and she just knew that they weren't in control of their own minds. They were slaves to Father Dagon.

If Maddie ever became a monster, she wanted it to be on her own terms.

"Children, rejoice!" The leader of the choir shouted over the abominable song. "You are remade in your Father's image, and now you shall meet him!"

Two of the men from the alcoves pulled open the huge metal barn doors, and suddenly the grotto was filled with the smell of seawater and the sound of crashing surf. Immediately, the gibbering, baying, croaking fish-frogs swarmed toward the water, and Maddie was carried along with them. She managed to take a deep breath right before they all plunged into the dark, surging waves.

Immediately, she lost her gorgeous red wig amongst the thrashing, splashing limbs. Maddie had never been a fast swimmer, but she had always been a strong one. It was hard to swim in her boots and poofy-sleeved shirt, hard to keep her head above water amidst the croaking throng surging out to sea, but she did it.

The throng thinned, and Maddie distantly glimpsed the sweeping spotlight in the lighthouse, which she remembered the bus passing. That way was town, and her parents' house. Safety.

She started to awkwardly breast-stroke toward the lighthouse, but something grabbed her. Hubert's awful croaking face loomed beside hers, his bulging eyes gleaming with mindless hunger.

Maddie shrieked and scrabbled her pirate's cutlass out of its scabbard and jabbed it at him, expecting it to uselessly break. Instead, she felt the blade sink into something soft. Hubert let out an inhuman barking cry and released her. She gave the sword another shove and let it go, too, splashing away as fast as she could.

He didn't follow.

Maddie staggered to shore on the rocky beach a few hundred yards north of the mansion. Her arms and legs were numb with cold. She was so exhausted she wanted to lie down and sleep, but she knew she couldn't. The people from the mansion could find her here, and she wasn't convinced that some of the fish-frogs wouldn't track her down. Besides, she'd learned about hypothermia in Girl Scouts, and if she didn't keep moving, she might get so cold she'd die. She sat down on a rock to pour the seawater out of her boots and wring out her socks as best she could. Her feet were wrinkled from her swim, and she had no doubt they'd be covered in the worst blisters she'd ever had by the time she got home.

She was elated to find that her iPhone was still in her vest pocket, and when she pulled it out, surprised to discover that the inexpensive case had protected it from the seawater. Her mood dropped when she realized that she didn't have any bars. She put her damp socks and boots back on and kept going down the beach, hoping that the rocky cliffs would end soon so she could get back onto the highway like her mom had told her.

"Like Mom told me," She repeated aloud to herself.

The sudden shock of realization made her stop and stand very still, shivering. Her mother had known this was going to happen. Maybe not *exactly* what had happened, but she knew *something* bad would happen. Why had she sent her to the party if she knew? Had her own mother betrayed her? Maddie felt a new surge of terror and anger. If her mother was in on this, could she still go home?

She shook her head, scolding herself. Her mom loved her. She *did*. But Maddie couldn't understand why her mom would send her into the mouth of horror when her entire life she'd kept Maddie away from anything and everything that seemed even slightly dangerous. But, she had . . . and Maddie figured her mother had some explaining to do. At *least*.

Further, even if Maddie did want to run away, where could she go? She didn't know how to contact any of her other relatives, and she didn't have any money for a bus. Maddie had seen enough thrillers to suspect a conspiracy, and she didn't know who could be trusted. If she couldn't trust her own mom, she certainly couldn't trust neighbors or teachers she'd only known for a few months, could she? There wasn't much choice except to go home.

Shivering in the fitful wind, she plodded along the dark beach, eyes downcast, until she smelled burning gasoline and glimpsed the flicker of flames in her peripheral vision. The Cosmic Cola bus had crashed over the guardrail onto its side and was burning. The whole thing was engulfed. Two firetrucks were vainly trying to put the flames out, and the local news SUV was filming a reporter a safe distance away.

This was how they were going to explain the kids' disappearance, she realized. A big tragic bus crash that people would forget in a decade or two. Probably if she looked in the town records, she'd find that some other terrible accident had befallen the kids picked for the big Devil's Night party thirty years before.

Left with no doubt whatsoever that this was a conspiracy, Maddie crept onward, making sure that she wouldn't be seen as she passed the crash.

Once she reached the highway, Maddie finally got some bars on her phone. She crouched behind a roadside bush, took a deep breath, and started composing a text to her mom's new number.

Hey I'm alive, she keyed.

She waited a few minutes, and then three dots began to throb on her screen.

Thank God. Are you ok?

Wet but ok, she texted back. *And the bus is on fire. Pick me up please?*

I'm so sorry but I can't leave. Steve took my keys. Don't go to the house. I'm in the gazebo at the park . . . can you make it?

Yes. Maddie wanted to punch her stepfather.

Good. Don't let anyone see you if you can help it.

She finally made it to the little park down the street from her parents' house in the early grey dawn when the sun was just a rumor below the horizon. Exhaustion had dissolved her rage and terror into a disbelieving numbness. Her mother was sitting in the white gazebo, dozing against a pillar, one of the jack-o-lanterns she'd helped Maddie carve sitting in her lap. Its candle had gone out. A wine glass and an empty bottle of merlot lay on the white-washed wooden planks beside her.

Maddie shrugged off the blanket she'd pilfered from a beach house clothesline and shook her mother's shoulder. "Mom."

Mrs. Gibbs woke with a start, briefly stared at Maddie as if she were a ghost, then leaped up and grabbed the girl in a strong hug. Maddie felt her anger melt as her mother softly wept into her hair and rocked her back and forth.

"Mom, I can't breathe . . . "

Her mother released her, looked around, and then pressed a finger to her lips. Her eyes were very red, as if she'd been crying a long time that night. "We have to be quiet. If anyone knows you're alive, they'll come after you again. I won't be able to do anything. I'm so sorry about all of this, honey."

"What the hell is going on?" Maddie whispered, then flinched, expecting her mother to scold her for using a swear word.

But her mother didn't even seem to notice. "There's a cult here, and it's real, and Steve was a part of it long before I met him. And now we're all sucked in. I'm so sorry."

Maddie felt her anger rise again. "Why didn't you tell me?"

Fresh tears welled in her mother's eyes. "I couldn't, honey. If you had known, you would have been so scared, and they'd have known that I told you. We'd both be dead now, and there would be nobody to protect your little brother and sister. I did the best I could think to do. I slipped Steve a Valium and tried to get us all out last week. I still didn't believe in magic. I thought it was all a bluff to scare me . . . but it's all real."

Her mother's gaze turned distant, and when she spoke again, her voice was hollow. "There was a ritual. I thought Steve and I were just going to lunch . . . but we weren't. They forced me. I'm bound here. I will literally die if I try to leave here. That's why Steve took my keys . . . he thinks I might try to drive off anyway, not caring if it kills me. He's probably right about that. He had to promise a child to Dagon so he could rise in the ranks of the Order. He promised you. And you're still promised."

God. This was even more awful than she had imagined. "What happens now?"

"You have to leave here, tonight, and never come back. If they think you drowned in the ocean, the Order considers the promise fulfilled even though Dagon didn't get another child. But if they find out you're alive, they'll try to get you. And if they can't get you, they'll demand that Steve give them a different child. And then he'll hand over your little brother or little sister."

Maddie felt a shock run from her skull to the soles of her aching feet. "He wouldn't. He loves them."

Her mother gave a short, quiet, bitter laugh. She looked terrified. "He would. He'd hand over all of us if they asked him to. And then he'd do his Prince Charming act for some other woman and they'd get married and start a new family. For now, he wants me alive because I'm useful to him. He's not at all the man I thought he was. He's not even the man *you* think he is, and I know you never liked him much."

"He's a *monster*," Maddie whispered.

Another quiet, bitter laugh. "This whole town is a monster factory, and it has been for a long, long time. But if you leave before they discover that you're alive, you and I and the twins stay safe. It's probably better if I don't know exactly where you are. I wish it didn't have to be this way, but it does."

Maddie felt completely lost. "Where do I go?"

Her mother sighed and put her face in her hands. "This is where I fail at motherhood. I don't have a clue where you can go, other than far away from here. I can give you a few hundred dollars in cash. That's maybe enough to travel with."

"Could I go live with Grandma?"

Her mom shook her head. "She's moving into an assisted living facility. And even if you could stay with her, I wouldn't trust her to keep you secret from Steve. She thinks the world of him."

"Oh." Maddie felt a lump rise in her throat. "Do I have any long-lost cousins out there?"

"None that I know of. I'm sorry, honey."

Her mother reached under the wooden gazebo bench and pulled out Maddie's purple backpack, which was absolutely stuffed full. It reminded her of a grape. "I packed up some clothes and other essentials for you. Things Steve won't notice being gone." She paused, starting to tear up again. "I didn't think to bring your violin. I'm sorry. I'll try to get it to you, somehow."

"It's okay, Mom." Maddie certainly had a whole lot more to worry about than missing practice.

Her mother broke down in deep, wracking sobs. "It's not okay. None of this is okay. I can't protect my own daughter. So many things could happen to you out there, and I can't stop any of them. I'm so sorry, baby."

Maddie had never seen her mother this hopeless and miserable before. She was crying like her whole world was coming to an end. The girl felt sick, scared, and didn't know what to do.

She nearly jumped when her phone vibrated in her vest pocket. A new text message? Who could be texting her? She pulled the phone out to check.

Maeve here. Saw the bus burning on the 11 pm news. If you made it out, I can help. LMK. I'm at the store all night.

"How'd she get my number?" Maddie breathed. Then she remembered. "Oh, right. I wrote it down on the costume rental contract."

Her mother regained some of her composure. "Who's that?"

"The lady at the store who picked out my pirate outfit. She says she can help me."

"That . . . that seems sketchy." Her mother shook her head, sniffling, wiping her eyes. "We can't trust anyone in Marsh Landing."

"She's not a townie, though."

Maddie bit her lip, staring at the text. Maeve had given her a flask so she wouldn't have to drink the hateful Cosmic Cola. And a sword she could actually use to defend herself! She'd given her the tools she needed to dodge the transformation and escape. "I wouldn't have survived the party without the things she rented me. I think she knew what was going to happen. I think we can trust her."

"I'm still worried that this could be a trap."

Maddie felt an intense spike of frustration. *Now* her mom was worrying about traps? "Nobody else is offering me any help. You said that you don't know where I can go. Maybe she does?"

Her mother took a trembling, deep breath. "Ok. Let's go see her. Together."

Halloween Beyond was dark except for a blue light way in the back of the store. Maddie tentatively pushed on the door and discovered it was unlocked.

Right after they stepped inside, her phone buzzed with a new text: *I'm in the back of the store. Follow the light and you'll find me.*

Maddie turned on her phone's flashlight and she and her

mother made their way through the maze of aisles to the back of the store toward the faint blue glow. The source of it always seemed to be just out of sight, as if they were following a ghost or will-o-the-wisp. It certainly wasn't close to the creepiest thing the girl had seen that night, but it made her shiver just the same.

They stepped under a broad archway made to look like interlocking oak branches, and followed the glow down a corridor where the three-dimensional tree branch decorations continued on the walls.

But right after the vinyl tiles beneath her feet suddenly became soft forest moss, Maddie realized the branches weren't fake at all, and that the glow was actually the moon shining over the tops of gently swaying trees.

Maddie heard her mom suck in her breath behind her and then mutter, "What the . . . "

"Hello, ladies." Maeve stepped out from behind the trunk of a broad oak. She was wearing a luminous gown that seemed to be made from pure moonlight. "I'm glad you chose to see me tonight."

Maddie heard her mother stumble backward a few steps. "This . . . this is Elfame." Her mother sounded astonished and afraid. "When I was little, my grandmother told me stories about the fairy folk, about this place. But I didn't believe her. You're sidhe." She spoke the word like an accusation.

Maeve's placid expression didn't change. She simply nodded. "Aye, it's true."

Her mom grabbed Maddie's hand and started to pull her back toward the corridor. "She's a trickster. A fairy sorceress. She's not *human*. We can't trust her."

"Wait." Maeve held up a graceful hand, and her mother paused. "I offer you no tricks this Samhain. I hope to offer a solution to your immediate problem that, in the long run, will benefit your world as well as mine."

"What do you mean?" asked Maddie.

"Dagon and his cultists are a threat to all of us. They won't stop at dominating and destroying the mortal realm. They want to end the sidhe as well. But you can help us all, Maddie Flynn."

"Me? How?"

"The lottery was a sham. A few of the children who lost their humanity this evening were random sacrificial victims, but the cult elders deliberately chose the rest of you. All of the Chosen had qualities that, if encouraged and properly nurtured, could threaten Dagon. But only you survived intact. And I intend to help you develop your talents to become exactly what that accursed sea god fears most."

"What are you proposing?" Her mom's voice shook.

"Maddie must serve as my apprentice for thirteen years. During that time, I will teach her magic and how to best do battle with Dagon and his ilk. I promise to be a fully dedicated instructor. Only a year shall pass in the mortal realm, and next Samhain she shall emerge as a woman, fully grown in body and powers."

"Are you actually giving her a choice?" her mother asked.

"I am. I cannot teach a student who is not willing to learn, so this must be her choice. But the alternative to my offer . . . isn't very good, is it?"

Maeve leveled a sad, direct gaze at Maddie. "The cult has had its eyes on you since you were born. They poisoned your father, gave him cancer, and sent Gibbs to seduce your mother once he was dead."

Her mother stifled a gasp and sob. The news rocked Maddie back on her heels, but part of her was not even slightly surprised. For the second time that evening, she felt grimly vindicated for disliking Steve from the start.

"And now," Maeve continued, "You face an uncertain future of hiding in the shadows, of being afraid, of being powerless against dark forces you don't understand. Is that what you'd rather have?"

"No. I want to learn to fight. I want to learn magic. I want to help my mom and Travis and Tiffany get away from Steve."

"But honey," her mom said. "You'll miss out on your teen years. No high school, no going to prom, no going to college . . . "

"How can I have any of those things if I'm hiding or homeless? My life can't be normal now, can it? But if I go with Maeve, at least it might matter."

Her mom was silent for a moment, head bowed.

"Okay," she finally said. "If this is what you want to do, I support it. I love you."

The gravity of the situation finally hit Maddie full force. She was going to leave, live in a strange world, and be gone longer than she'd been alive. There was the chance she might never see her mother again. She started to tear up. "I love you, too, Mom."

Her mother gave her a long hug. "A day won't pass where I don't think of you. Be good, and be strong."

"I will." Maddie released her mother, straightened her spine, and faced Maeve. "I'm ready."

The sidhe queen smiled at her. "Wonderful. My realm has needed some new blood for a long time. Follow me. I have so much to show you . . ."

A GENTLEMAN'S SUIT

KATE MARUYAMA

For Miguel Rosales and the Halloween Gang

ACKNOWLEDGEMENTS

Thanks, first of all, to Lisa Morton for the opportunity and Lucy Snyder for the community spirit, I am grateful to share this world with these two brilliant writers.

Thanks to Miguel Rosales, "Mikeween" who makes every Halloween the best for us (and no, you do not have to buy the Death on a boat animatronic because of the book), to Valerie Riddel and Gloria Villegas for the company, the wine, and the stories we've gathered. A huge thank you the Halloween gang, Mireya and Ben Rosales, Daniel Mariscal, Christian and Krista Villegas, and, of course, our own Jack and Reed Maruyama for sharing the stories that allowed me to litter this thing with Easter eggs (mini pumpkins?) that I hope makes this book fun for you, and proof of the best Halloweens in the best neighborhood for the holiday. And thanks to whoever that kid was with the awesome jellyfish costume.

Thank you to Dale Weatherwax Hanes for their swiftest and kindest sensitivity read.

To Joe Mynhardt and the team at Crystal Lake, for all you do.

And thanks to Ko, for everything every day, and always.

HALLOWEEN IS A high holiday in our house, and my dad is the King of Halloween.

I was going to sit out this trip to a Halloween store and stay home to work on my college applications. But Mom was anxious and bribed me with twenty bucks and a whispered promise to get me the new skateboard I'd been eyeing for almost a year now. She said, "Lex, just. Just make sure your dad doesn't spend too much, okay? I don't want him dipping into your college fund, and we definitely have enough shit." She waved her arm in the direction of the garage which we both knew was chockablock with Halloween stuff: a styrofoam graveyard, skeletons rising up, an enormous spider web, a giant spider for over the door, and more importantly, about fifteen animatronic beasties, from the terrifying clown jack-in-the-box who bobbed up and down leering, to the witch, crone version, stirring a cauldron we lit on Halloween night and blew fog out of, to a skeleton dancing ghoulishly in its electric chair, to Sarah, an animatronic ghoul mother rocking her ghoulish baby Tim in a rocking chair, comforting him, "You're safe with Mama, you're safe with me baby."

And the giant flaming pumpkin. But I'll get back to that. All the stuff waited in the loft of our garage for the hottest day of the year for us to get it out and set it up.

Halloween was my favorite, and our neighborhood was the absolute best. With the streets packed with kids and over-the-top displays on every front lawn, from the moment the sun set on the 31st, it was a block party that took over our entire corner of the city. And Dad, Roberto the King of Halloween, had the most elaborate display which he'd been perfecting for years since before any of his kids were born. I always got amped up for Halloween, and I was most proud of our haunted front lawn, which drew a crowd. Even in my jaded junior high years, it was the best holiday. Now that I was a senior in high school, I should really be past it all, right? But sexy vampire costumes and make-out parties with heavy drinking and everyone getting baked was all that was going on with the high school crowd.

Nope. Not for me. Halloween? Give me this street on that magic night and dozens of kids jumping and screaming at the demonic jack-in-the-box clown. Give me eight million bags to put candy into. And my dad in his element. I craved it even more this year, my last at home and our first back after last year's depressing quarantine. I wanted Dad and the neighborhood to reclaim the day.

But, yeah, the guy had a spending problem and Mom knew that a trip to the store for more lights and spiderweb and, "I have to get some candy anyway," meant we'd likely be coming home a few hundred bucks poorer with something ungodly in the trunk. Especially since this was his first time back. There might be some hope if we made him bring the Camry. If he brought the truck, it would all be over.

Because, worse still, this was a *new* Halloween store. A pop-up down on Magnolia that Dad had seen on some fliers. "Don't you just love the name, Lex?" He held up both his hands and grinned wide, as he pulled them apart . . . if I were an animator, I'd put the words between his hands in vibrating 3D. He said, "*Halloween Beyond*. Like beyond! I mean we got Halloween here, but we're gonna go . . . " his eyes lit up again and he almost growled the word, "*beyond*." He laughed a high gleeful chuckle he saved for mischief and nodded and made his eyes go googly.

"Okay, Dad." I tried to act as blasé as I could to live up to my teen misanthrope personality, but I had to admit his glee was contagious. "Can we go now? I want to get back to work on my college apps." I knew a Halloween store was at least an hour and a *new* Halloween Store meant a good two. I was happy to hang with him, but time was a concern.

"Right! Right. Okay. Here we go."

I tried to convince him I wanted to practice driving the Camry, which would guarantee no enormous purchases.

Dad said, "No, no, I'll drive, let's take the pickup."

I saw Mom's look of despair as she heard this. I winked at her, like *I got this*. But we both knew I was helpless to face The King of Halloween when he was in full throttle. Something about the way he whistled, spun his keys on his finger, and trotted out the door let us know resistance was futile.

Any worry and tension I was carrying lifted as we traveled down our street. I loved this old Bronco with its smells of baked

Naugahyde, diesel fumes, and adventure. We rattled down out of our hills of super 1930s suburban-looking streets. We had a nice little one-story house, not like the mansions further up the street, but comfortable. I shared a room with my kid sister Maria, who in fourth grade was becoming a pain in the butt, but I loved her. My brother Mike had his own room down the hall, and we didn't see him much once he hit twelve two years ago.

My dad whacked my knee when we crossed over the 5 and into the city storefronts of Burbank as we rolled down Magnolia Blvd. "Lex, Lex, my Halloween Hex." In Halloweenville, Hex was a compliment.

I laughed. It was a nice cool morning, the first in a while and for mid-October in LA which was usually hot as Hades, it felt like a gift. Windows down, Dad and I kept good company. He was easy to be quiet with. I was going to miss these Saturdays. I already missed my lifelong best friend Duncan coming along on these trips. Three years since he ghosted me, and it still stung. *Screw that guy.*

We drove past familiar restaurants and stores including Halloween Town where I'd spent many hours of my childhood, then Dad pulled over and we were in front of one of those 1950s storefronts that I'd sworn had a florist in it just last week when I was down here thrifting. A large orange sign hung above the entryway, with *Halloween Beyond* written across in black. It was framed on one side and the top by a black silhouette of a barren oak tree, an owl on its branches.

Dad squinted up at the front and the sign.

He said now with a musing tone of admiration, "Halloween Beyond . . . " That chuckle again. Then, again, "Beyond."

He wasn't letting this one go. I laughed as we masked up and got out of the car.

DEATH

This boat and the trip back and forth, commuting souls, this is what I do. This is all I do, really. It does get dreary.

First thing, people are always disappointed to see me. I like to chat, see, but they come through that tunnel and see me, take a good look around at the black, black river, at the cavern that is rocky and brown and fades into infinite blackness above, they see the one lantern on my boat, and they are mostly afraid. I admit, my tall form, skeleton head, and giant black cloak make me kind of intimidating. I always have to wait while they turn around and try to run back through the tunnel. I swear, nine times out of ten this happens, they try to run back, and I can count it out, "5, 6, 7 . . . " before they skid to a halt right in front of me again. Sometimes I try to talk them out of the running part, but honestly, it takes less energy waiting for them to get back to me, defeated.

When the dead finally face facts, pay their fare, and get onboard, I try striking up a conversation. I like to hear what's going on in their realm. It's all interesting. At first, I tried asking big questions, "So what do you mean iron horse?" but after several decades, I realized it's just better to ask people about themselves because when people talk about themselves, they tend to go into more detail. While most folks sit and sob, or are in a stunned silence, some are nervous talkers. That's where I pick things up. I learned about the internet this way. This one guy, a big gamer I'm guessing, met someone on the line. On the inline? Anyway, it didn't end well, so he . . . well, I'm not supposed to talk about these things, but you should know that he chose to get on that boat.

The talkers are few and far between. Mostly it's me and the boat, and the water, and that trip to the afterlife, Hades, whatever your belief system allows you to call it. I am Death or Charon, depending on who's talking. But I promise you this, it ends the same way for all of you. You may spend your whole life dodging me, trying to buy enough things to keep me at bay, you can run miles every day of your life, eat the best foods. At the end? Same story. Me, the boat, the crossing.

It gets pretty repetitive, that swish of the paddle, the sobs, the wailing, and you know, sometimes the talker who has to 'splain about his job and all the people in it. That's the sort of pointless stuff people put their life energy into.

Then *she* comes through that tunnel, confident and determined, all what, five foot two of her? Drowning in that massive shimmering cloak of gray and blue and black, her forest of blonde hair cascades in sharp relief and her pale, pale face takes me aback. I recognize her from somewhere, this quiet, thoughtful, *young? old?* woman. She doesn't speak at first, so I figure I've got the non-talker and we settle into the journey. I row slowly and try to keep the paddle from splashing. There's something serious about her, and I like the look of her face, her eyes green, her skin pale and even. *I know her. Why do I know her?*

She starts speaking so quietly, I can hardly hear her. And then her voice swells to fill the story. She tells me about her last encounter with humans. Two sisters, some woods, the thinning of the veil, and how close she'd gotten. How it made her think about being trapped. How it made her think about me. And then she talks about this shop. This changeable Halloween store. And she tells me how this store thrives on Halloween and how that flood of belief, combined with its magical properties, and about the veil's fragility at that time of year . . . the veil becomes thinner then and especially there.

I stop the boat. I say, because I knew it or I remember it, I'm not sure which, I say, "You aren't dead." I feel a weird kinship with her. If immortality is a space, then she is a fellow traveler.

She says, "No, just visiting. Why did you stop?" She is clear and loud, but there is a tone to her voice that lets me know she knows full well why I stopped.

I say, "I know you." It isn't an affection for her I have, it's a familiarity, a memory, a distant ring of a bell. Being familiar with someone was so foreign to me that it did almost feel like affection. But in looking at her longer, there is something about her. Something happened to me because of her. I can't remember. I know I want to get out of this place. And that she will lead the way.

I steer the boat in a different direction and say, "Tell me more about this store, this Halloween Beyond."

She says, "I think this may be the opportunity you've been looking for."

LEX

Living with my dad, you get to know all the Halloween stores. The pop-ups are the most fun—sometimes they pop up in mini-malls, sometimes next to the basement of Ralphs Grocery. They always seem a bit out of place, but you can count on the displays being fantastic. I remember when the Burbank Ikea moved, and they used the old building for a Halloween store. It was odd walking into a space that used to be home furnishings and lingonberry jam to find that spooky clown jack-in-the-box cackling at you. Yep, that's where we got it. But the strangest part—they had hung up black tarps to create walls at the edge of the warehouse. The fabric sagged and split in spaces. The light hit only a foot or two into the space and then there was darkness. The black vastness beyond was scarier than any animatronic headless bloody little girl. I imagined you could play a hell of a game of flashlight tag there. But when I thought about those deep and broad endless aisles where we'd gotten our kitchen chairs, our plates, Christmas gifts for my cousins going to college, when I thought of the endlessness of that warehouse all in windowless darkness, that stopped me.

I can take any cursing witches, projections, headless horsemen, scary clowns, or living dolls with hollowed out eyes. But I cannot abide complete darkness.

Halloween Beyond looked cozy and small from the outside. Inside its 20th century-style shop window, an animatronic clown stabbed at a pumpkinhead figure. The display was clever. Sometimes the stores just set the different pieces up in a row doing their own thing, but this window dresser had angled the clown so the stabbing looked like it was making contact, and they tilted the pumpkinhead just enough away that you couldn't see the contact made. There were body parts littering the ground beneath their feet. Over in the corner a crone version witch (I have Wiccan friends and bruja friends, so I try to be specific about how I say these things) was bent over a Ouija board and a Wednesday Adams-looking dead girl watched with liquid black eyes. By the time I looked up from the display, Dad had disappeared inside.

I opened the shop door, which sported a glass pane where they'd hung an old curtain. A blood scrawled sign read *Halloween Beyond: Enter if you Dare.* Of course, there was a loud cackle in my ear and a wind-up bat swooped over my head. Two steps forward and, predictably, that Jack-in-the-box clown popped out at me, leering in my face. It was like seeing an old friend.

Dad was nowhere to be seen. Ahead of me lay a maze of costumes on racks, pirates, princesses, sexy nurses, and my pet peeve, sexy Freddy Krueger and sexy Jason. The usual fare hung in their plastic bags with photos of the contents displayed. But unlike every other store we'd been into, beyond those first racks were more racks with legit costumes. I knew Dad would be here all day, so I went straight along the aisle running my hands along sleeves upon sleeves in black coats and jackets. Duncan would frickin' love this place. *Don't think about him. His choice. His loss.*

I started flicking through the rack and saw a pirate costume complete with wooden leg and a parrot sewn on the collar, real Freddy Krueger complete with bloodstained sweater; his metal claw glove hanging from the neck of the hanger clinked as I moved it. I reached out to touch the blades expecting clever plastic, but they were metal, cold, and hard. I wondered what kind of lawsuit you could file with that costume. I leafed further and found the best, the absolute best 19th century gentleman's suit that would look killer on me complete with a dark green waistcoat brocaded with twining green vines and leaves, gold thread running throughout to highlight the edges, a beautifully tailored black jacket with matching trousers, and a high collared shirt. A collapsible top hat and a cravat hung from the neck of the costume in a bag. I fished around the neck and the sleeves for a price tag, but couldn't find one. I heaved it off the hanger and it crackled with static. It smelled like ozone and something from long ago. Not stale, just different.

The row of antique costumes went on for what seemed like farther than the store could reach. I walked through racks of princesses, wizards, witches, period army pieces, knights with real chain mail. I called out, "Dad?"

An enthusiastic, "Halloween *Beyond*!" echoed from somewhere I couldn't see followed by his wicked laugh. I knew we were in trouble in this place. This was the kinda place Dad might rent a trailer for, like he did that time we had to get three animatronic things in one year. Mom said it was the year he lost his mind because she'd had another kid. He took Maria's unplanned arrival as a license to an endless childhood.

The costumes opened up into a section at the back with a long glass counter filled with all kinds of creepy and fun things. There were some display costumes hung on the wall, and behind the counter a very wide doorway was framed by a wizened oak tree so well done you couldn't tell if it was real, or papier mâché, or resin. The doorway was covered by a tarp, and the room behind it was so black that it reminded me of that abandoned Ikea. I knew these shops on Magnolia Blvd, I'd been into dozens of them repeatedly. I knew the depth they should have, the width, and like how far back the bathroom was. But this place, I felt like I'd walked a city block to get to that counter at the rear.

"Lex!" Dad's voice came from the opposite direction I thought it would. He was over to my left at the end of an aisle where some of the larger animatronic figures stood in a row against a wall. Oh, for god's sake he was standing in front of a life-size . . . no, seven-foot-tall figure of Death. But it wasn't just another figurine. Damned if Death wasn't standing at the back of a full-sized boat with room enough to seat two. Dad was sitting in the boat, Death looming over him, and he spread his arms wide with that trademark grin. He said, "Right??? I mean, how could we not?"

Mom was gonna kill me.

"How much is it?" I tried to use Mom's warning tone, to ring a bell, some sort of caution in him, but he wouldn't bite.

Trademark grin, he said, "Never you mind about that. Help me find someone who works here."

I know it was only October 5th, but still, it was a Saturday, and this was Magnolia Blvd, and you'd think there'd be *someone* around the place. I left Dad sitting with Death and went back to the counter with that twisted tree behind it. "Hello?" With the size of Death and the boat, I knew getting it into the truck was going to take negotiating and time. It seemed like the more expensive the item, the longer the dealing with the clerk took, so I wanted us to get help as soon as possible.

My second Personal Inquiry Question for the UC applications was driving me nuts. Four chunky essays I had to write about myself. *Four.* I wondered if I could write about Halloween. I had already written about my concussion my sophomore year that accounted for my dip in grades, I'd written about my swimming and a third about how no one can just let you be when you're non-binary and mixed, but I needed something less serious, fun for the fourth one. I had a feeling I'd open the essay with Dad sitting in the boat in front of Death. That'd grab them. But now that I'd figured it out, I wanted to get home to work on it.

I leaned over the glass counter trying to see in the dark space beyond the curtain. "Hello?" It took a full minute of calling before a woman emerged from the darkness.

I feel like 'woman' wasn't enough of a word for this crazy, tiny, beautiful being. Her hair was a many-hued blonde and her skin so pale and luminous it made me think of vampires or the airbrushed ladies in perfume ads. Her eyes were a swirling, almost changeable ocean green, and I couldn't be sure, but my immediate impression was that she and the tree were somehow . . . connected? She was wearing a forest green N-95 mask and I wondered where I could score one to go with my costume. The moment she saw me, her eyes lit up like she knew me, which made me feel emboldened and horribly awkward all at once. She said, "Can I help you? I see you've found the right costume." Her voice, tinged with a light Irish accent, was vibrant and stirred something in me—freedom and the future. It resonated with possibility.

"Yes, thank you!" I learned a while back that if you're super friendly and immediate upfront, people don't ask the annoying questions. The most common question in my life was, "What are you?" and I never knew if they were asking about my race or my gender. Friendliness didn't always work in grammar school when I was the Mad Hatter or decided to be Dream from *Sandman*. But real Halloween people? Those who work at these stores? They usually met you where you were for who you were. And Maeve (her plastic nametag was attached to her incongruous bright orange Halloween Apron) was kind of beyond that. The look in her eyes let me know that she saw me, Lex.

I cleared my throat and looked back down to the costume I was holding. "Hi, can you tell me the price on this one? And also, we um . . . my dad wants to buy Death on a boat."

Her knowing smile lit me up inside. This was a proper Halloween person. Halloween . . . *Beyond*. She picked up the suit and looked at it fondly. She said, "You found exactly the right costume for you. I'll help your father with Death, but this will be five dollars. Return it by Monday."

"Excuse me?" When she said five, I was waiting for the zero to follow, waiting to be shocked.

The smile was real, "Five dollars."

I pulled my wallet out of my back pocket, pulled out a five, and put it on the counter. "Don't you need a deposit or something?" I was just a rascal teenager, who's to say I wouldn't bolt with this thing?

She gazed into what must have been wide eyes, considering. There was something older than her years in that green. An old soul maybe. She said, "I'll have your Dad's credit card for Death, won't I?"

I laughed. Death made everything funnier it seemed. Maeve was off with an unusual speed. I hoisted my costume and hustled behind. Dad was crouched behind Death now, peering into his animatronic controls which must be in his back. Death's robes were over Dad's head making it look like it had a bustle. Dad really was only proving my point about the hilarity. Not hilarious was the $399 price tag I saw dangling from the cloak. Mom *was* going to kill me.

With a hissing noise, the cloaked skeleton figure jumped to life, pushing his stick/paddle/ whatever that was alongside the boat and lifting it once it got behind him. It could be a stick if he were punting or they could have cut the oar off because, front lawn, you know? Once he finished the cycle, he lifted the stick and rowed again.

Dad said, "I got Death working!" He laughed and rubbed his hands and stepped out of the boat in time to hear Death say, "Your time has come. Two coins to cross. Get into the boat." The voice was warbly and deep, electronic, and seemed to come from somewhere in his chest and not his head.

Dad laughed a "Heeeee!" and turned to Maeve, eyes wild. "We'll take him!"

I felt like Maeve was my cool friend and Dad was going to embarrass me, but Maeve said, "I was hoping you'd come today, Beto. And I was hoping you'd say that. This is the perfect piece for your display."

I don't know why her moderately stalkery salesperson talk didn't bug me, but her voice, how she was, felt completely genuine. Dad had his Halloween glee on, and she was feeding it, so there was no stopping them.

I said, "Death on the boat, huh? River Styx?"

She looked at the figure, considering for a moment. "It's meant to be Charon on the Styx, but myths and legends are sometimes just specific cultural lenses, human inklings of what's real." She walked over to the frozen figure and laid her hand on his shoulder. "I have a feeling this representation is correct."

Death kicked into action again, rowing, saying, "Your time has come. Two coins to cross. Get into the boat."

Maeve said, "That voice though. That's definitely not right." Again, that knowing tone. Like she and Death hung out or something. She turned to my dad saying, "Just this?"

He blushed a little, flustered and said, "My wife didn't want me to spend much and this. Well. It's kind of my limit."

Maeve chuckled. "I didn't mean to be pushy. I just need to ring it up."

He laughed, relieved. "Yes, okay." He eyed me and said, "Unless . . . Lex, did you want that costume?" He turned to Maeve, "They always find the coolest thing. This kid's got an eye, I can tell you."

My heart swelled a bit. Embarrassing Dad was making me shine. I was ashamed for being embarrassed in the first place. Plus, he always used my correct pronouns. No questions from him. My classmates and sibs were harder to bring on board.

Maeve said, "They paid for it already."

Dad's eyes lit up with pride. "Of course they did."

Maeve said, "I'll get the guys to load up your car while you pay. I think Lex has got other stuff to do today." Okay. Weird. Maybe because I was a teenager, and it was a Saturday? Maybe she saw my impatience? Maeve took the costume from my hands. "Pick it up Halloween afternoon. I'll have it dry cleaned by then." She grinned, "You'll have a spectacular Halloween with this one, I just know it."

Sure enough, when we got to the truck, Death was all boxed and loaded. The picture on the outside made it look smaller somehow. This was going to be quite the ordeal to set up.

As we buckled in, I said, "Hey, Dad. Can I work for a couple of hours and then help you later this afternoon?"

He put his hand on the back of my neck and squeezed like he'd done all my life. I loved that life-affirming *my kid* feeling it gave me. He said, "I think your sibs can do a little training this year. After all, next year we'll be doing all this without you."

All the excitement and fear I had around college and future and forward had my heart quailing again. I said, "Three o'clock. I'll show them the ropes." No way Maria and Mike were going to bogart my last Halloween setup.

We pulled into the driveway and both kids came bouncing out of the house. Dad sniffed the air, "Wind's changing." The cool onshore flow had shifted to a nose pricking dry offshore breeze that threatened to heat the day up real quick. October weather was a guessing game in Los Angeles, day to day, hour to hour.

I had to laugh. "Of course, it's going to be hot. It's attic time." We never, ever got to bring things out of the attic for Halloween on a cool day. Why should today be any different?

That afternoon, with Maria turning cartwheels in the yard and being no help at all and twelve-year-old Mike working with a concentrated intensity, we got Death put together, standing upright in his boat and functioning. It was clear Mike would be my Halloween setup successor. I didn't know how he'd cope with Dad's fervor, especially in organizing crap in the attic. I knew Dad could get cranky, but I was old enough to give as much shit as I was getting, and we usually turned it into a comedy routine where we'd roast each other. He'd rib me for being no help at all (while I was doing everything) and I'd bust on him for losing it over the smallest of things. Mike was moodier than I was, so it was likely going to be a little stormier up there in the attic on the hottest day of next year. But I guess none of it was going to be my problem then, anyway.

Mom was at work all day, so when she got home, it would all be up. The graveyard, the Jack-in-the-box clown, the witches, the skeletons. We angled Death's boat in the smaller patch of lawn to the right of our curvy front walk. He would ride between the flaming pumpkin, which was kept in the driveway for the fire hazard part (details on that later, promise), and the sidewalk. Death stood back toward the house, but still impressive. It looked as if his boat would join the stream of the sidewalk and come for anyone who approached.

I loved putting the animatronics together best, these old familiar characters. Soon we had Sarah the dead mother, and her baby Tim set up in their rocking chair, her saying, "Oh my darling, you're safe with Mama, you're safe with me baby." She was hella creepy when we got her, but after six years of assembling her and getting her rocking, she'd become another member of the family. Maria sat next to Sarah and said all her dialogue with her, and their chorus made the whole thing creepier. Mike liked imitating the jack-in-the-box's scary cackle.

That afternoon we'd gotten through a whole tray of Halloween orange Oreos, so Mike and Maria were bouncing off the walls, jumping around and screaming despite the heat. We collapsed in a heap on the front lawn, to get a breather. Dad had gone back to the Halloween store because there was a stack of foam jack o'lanterns he heard were on sale.

The day had gotten hot and sweaty, and my knee was throbbing where I'd scraped it on something in the attic, but the shade of the house was hitting in a spot behind the graveyard and it was nice to sit somewhere halfway cool, among the tangle of electrical cords that formed their own spiderweb on the front lawn. Maria slammed against my back and threw her arms around me.

We called our cauldron-stirring witch Griselda, and always speculated what her brew could do. Mike said, "This year Griselda's going to make me fly."

Maria, too hot on my back, hugging too hard on my neck said, "This year Griselda's gonna make me cry. Cuz it's the last Halloween with Lex."

My eyes pricked and I hugged her back for a moment before wrestling her to the ground to tickle her. Big sibs had to live up to our names after all. I said, "This year, Griselda's gonna make me . . . " High would rhyme, and made me laugh, but these two were mercifully still kids. "Pie," I said.

Mike said, "Mmm . . . pumpkin pie."

Maria said, "Why we gotta wait 'til Thanksgiving for that?"

Mike said, "Because we're using the pumpkins right now." He waved to the twelve pumpkins placed in front of Death's boat. They'd remain whole until Halloween day when we'd carve them all. And I'd have to have my Cal State apps in, and my UCs lined up to go by then. Ugh this year. I was all choked up and sad one minute, super excited the next, weighed down another. And I had the SATs *again* the week after Halloween. I was supposed to be studying for those, like, now.

"Aaargh!" I fell back on the grass which was still warm from the pre-shadow sun, and I stared up at that extra blue October Los Angeles sky, the air crackling with static. I stank a little from my efforts in the attic, but Mike was seventh grade stinky, the kind that saturates their hair. Maria didn't stink yet. I wish I was that age again. You did what they had you do in school every day. No added responsibilities. No job. Your weekends were your own and Halloween meant a pillowcase full of enough candy to last you through Christmas season at school.

None of this was the same without Duncan. Why was everything so sad today? Not sad, just, like happy-sad, like kind of everything at once? Today was an everything day and I had no one to grumble about it with. Duncan had been good for everything days.

Duncan and I were thick as thieves from that first day we met in kindergarten. Best friends. We loved all the same things, all the time. Climbing trees in the park, biking, hiking with our parents who were good friends for a while there, comic books, and drawing. We loved getting our costumes together for Halloween like MONTHS ahead of time. Usually in August we'd have a meeting in his room at his parents' house (only two blocks away!) no grownups allowed, no outside friends allowed, and we'd launch our official Halloween (insert year here in big block numbers) planning session. When we were super little, it was all about candy. Around second grade it became costume planning. Third and fourth were all about trick or treating routes to maximize that candy. We both also had to have secret hiding places for the candy so our moms wouldn't find our chocolate. Around fifth grade it became pranks for certain neighbors or classmates' houses. On Halloween of 2015, we rigged this master spider attack to prank this really snotty girl named Kristen. Around 9 o'clock that Halloween night, you could hear her screams throughout all of Glendale, and didn't we laugh?

Duncan was the kind of guy where we could hang quietly all day doing our own thing. He was always drawing in his sketchbook. And his shoes were a mass of Sharpie characters and lines. But somewhere around seventh grade things changed. His parents got divorced and he moved out of his house into a tiny apartment in Los Feliz. Mom was super worried about him and his mom, so we dropped by a bunch, met them for dinner sometimes. Something was going on with his dad . . . missing money or something. It was a mystery talked about in low voices by our mothers, but any questions I asked Duncan, his mom, or my mom got shut down so hard I realized the topic was forbidden. I worked on just being there with my best friend, which was hard with whatever this secret was, and he wasn't talking much anyway. Our comfortable silences became awkward, and our visits felt long and uncomfortable. Later that summer, he ghosted me hard. The more I texted, the less he did until he stopped. It hurt a lot. I ended up stewing and spent the summer in the house reading books and moping.

The next year was high school, a whole new ballgame and I was so happy when I ran into Duncan in the hall. He looked different, paler with rings under his eyes. He had dyed his light brown hair a dark black.

I tried to be as cool as I could like he hadn't totally abandoned me. I said, "Hey, cool jacket." It was like a 1950s men's suit jacket. He had some vintage band's t-shirt on underneath it. I was happy to see his customary Converse covered with his drawings, that was something of the old him.

He didn't smile when he saw me. This hit me somewhere in the gut. He said, "Hey, Lex."

"How are you doing?" I felt like an ass for trying to put so much emotion into this tiny question.

He looked like he was formulating an answer when two other guys dressed just like him, one of them the class burnout, Charlie, showed up and gave him a nose-nod of a greeting. Not even apologetic, Duncan said, "Gotta go." He fell in with them and they were off down the hall.

Once you hang with a burnout, I guess you become one? Because after he met Charlie, they were rarely apart, and Duncan's new thing was hanging out in the wrong part of the schoolyard doing edibles between classes. Even though I was ready to be cool with it, I wasn't welcome to hang with him. It all made me so sad, especially the first Halloween without him. My friends Bella and Josie knew I was bummed, so they amped up the excitement for me that year, showing up early to help out with the twelve jack o'lanterns for the front yard, and with the fingers in a blanket, and basically making things less miserable for me. I loved them, but there was this Duncan-shaped hole in my days that loomed extra large around Halloween. Plus, I was worried about him.

That January I ran into Duncan in gym class and his pupils were so dilated it looked like he could see ghosts.

"Hey, Duncan."

It took him a moment to recognize me. He said, "Oh, hey, Lex! Guys this is Lex," but he turned around to find no one standing behind him. "They were just there, I swear."

He was so gone I wanted to cry. I said, "You know, you can still come to my house this Halloween. Any Halloween."

"Halloween, maaaan! How's Don Roberto the King of Halloween?"

I flushed with the familiarity and said, "Three more animatronics this year. We got this horrible Jack-in-the-box clown thingy, it'll scare the crap out of you."

"Daaaamnnnnn, I'll have to check that out." He nodded, staring into space, and I knew he'd never come over.

I said, "Well, man, you take care now."

"Yes! I'll take GOOD care! You take GOOD care too, Lex!" and he laughed which only underlined how nothing he'd said was funny.

I had a sudden need to get to Algebra and away from him.

Before I could go into a full wallow, Mike jumped on me and tackled me, and Maria dogpiled and soon we were laughing and rolling on the lawn until their elbows and weight started getting to me. "Get off, man!" I tried, once again, to let the bummer of Duncan go and revel in what was in front of me. I tossed them both on their backs and when we finally untangled, Mom was standing on the sidewalk in front of us. She dropped the groceries and something inside the bag broke with a *crack*. "Oh, for God's sake, Beto. What the hell, Lex?" She looked at me, furious, and nodded to Death, "You had one job."

I shrugged and said, "Dad's gonna Dad. It is Halloween after all."

DEATH

The days and crossings are different now, the edge taken off by something like hope. It has been so long since I've felt it, that I hardly recognize it. A day off, a chance to walk in the before. In the world where my love once walked with me. I can't remember much, everything is still beyond my grasp, but I do remember that love.

I didn't know how much I needed a break in my centuries, a millennium on that river, collecting coins, listening to people complain about the passing of their lives. Maeve pointed the way and now I wait for All Hallow's Eve to get through.

LEX

Death stood on the front lawn for the rest of the month.

Around the night of the 28th, I sat in bed staring at the UC questionnaire on my laptop. Every single question made me feel stupid and looking at my answers now, my nonbinary Personal Inquiry essay felt like a fraud. I'm not special. So many other people applying had legitimate stuff to talk about. I was just a coddled suburbanite whose parents supported them and whose Dad just bought a 400 dollar plastic animatronic version of Death.

No good sleeping tonight anyway, the Santa Anas were blowing in gusts and stops. In quiet moments, Maria's soft kidsnore calmed me a little, but I was getting increasingly angsty as the questionnaire proceeded. I got to *major?* With a million boxes to choose from. I looked at all the options and subsections trying to picture myself in any of these roles. I didn't know what I wanted to *be.* I had all these together classmates who were going into health care, or psychology, or wanted to be a lawyer or an engineer or something. I mean, I'm only eighteen, how am I supposed to figure that out? I was applying undeclared. I liked books. I liked making up stories. I liked history okay. I could declare history, but my guidance counselor said undeclared might get me farther and I didn't want to be pigeonholed. I was well acquainted with not wanting to be labeled, but Undeclared sounded like I wasn't formed yet. I wasn't fully me. And that gave me a nervous pit in my stomach.

Our whole time in high school my teachers were all push, push, push about college. My mom was chill, "It'll all work out," and kept me together with snacks and meals. My dad wasn't really worried. He would shrug and say, "As long as you're happy I don't care what you do." Ugh, even telling you this, I feel like I'm being boring. Restless and boring and undeclared. I mean I knew I was Lex, kid of Carol and Roberto. I knew I loved my family. But what do you want to *be*? Was a question I felt like I wouldn't have the answer to until I'd been out there in the world a little.

Next question: Family income for the past two years. Are you kidding me? I closed the laptop and figured I'd stewed enough for tonight. Then I thought of how stupid and selfish I was. Mom and Dad could afford to send me to college with only a few loans. Duncan wasn't able to go anywhere. His mom had sold their big house to pay for their day-to-day when his Dad bailed on them . . . trouble was he siphoned off their savings before they could see what happened and he skipped town. Being cranky over my college applications was basically being a privileged asshole. Not that Duncan could get anywhere with his burnout grades anyway.

I closed my eyes and listened to Maria's snoring. That usually soothed me to sleep. What was I going to do next year? In a room with a stranger. What if they didn't snore? And I'd have to answer questions. Or maybe they were a total phobe. Or a bully. Or a . . .

The window next to my bed rattled as the branches of the orange tree outside scuffled against it. There were soft thuds as the oranges hit the glass, and a sudden howl of wind made me clamp my mouth shut so as not to yell suddenly. Cuz, damn. I realized I was panic breathing, so I tried to slow my heart rate down, but by the time I quieted myself, it was too late. That shot of adrenaline had me vibrating with a kid level fear I hadn't felt in at least a decade.

I may not be able to decide on a major, but I could pick some frickin' oranges so that noise wouldn't happen again. As I crept out of our room, I closed the door gently behind me and moved down the hall as quietly as I could. I stepped really far to the left to avoid the squeaky board outside Mom and Dad's room and far to the right when I got outside Mike's room.

There was enough light from the streetlamps shining through the house for me to find my way out back, but I turned on the phone flashlight to navigate the yard. Again, I'm not so good with the dark. And it was *dark*. Usually, the pollution or the marine layer lit the sky up with orange from the tungsten lamps, but tonight the Santa Anas blew the sky clear. I looked up and saw the stars twinkling and my nose pricked with the strangely warm, dry wind. Everything rustled around me, and I was unprotected, exposed. I heard the thud of the oranges on the glass again, so I picked up the pruning clippers from the back table and beelined it to the side yard between our house and the neighbor's before I had time to totally freak myself out. The dark tonight, after all, was very dark. I had to turn sideways to skirt our orange tree, which was wedged in between our house and the fence. Its branches didn't have many places to go.

The wind stopped as suddenly as it had started. That was the weird part about the Santa Anas, it could be as quiet as it was noisy a moment before. My panicked breathing sounded ridiculous in the quiet.

I pulled the oranges off first. There were about five of them, too green to pick, so they took some twisting. Without the weight of the oranges, the branch lifted a little, so it wasn't against the window. Problem solved. But another gust turned that scuffling into a rattle as branches swayed and hit the window. I shone my light on the branch and aimed it back toward its source on the tree. I could cut it in three places and stop this nonsense right now.

The wind stopped again as I clipped one of the branches, and then another. But in the quiet came a most unusual sound for this dry time of year, one of water, running? Lapping? Flowing? The kind of sound you'd have to wait for a serious January rain to get around here . . . or a broken pipe. The sound was coming from out front. I hoped it wasn't a broken sprinkler or something. Dad's animatronics would be ruined.

I cut through the side gate and went straight for the street, that's usually where runaway water got to, but there was just a trickle. I followed the noise up to our front lawn where I saw Death, on his boat. As I stepped toward him, my flip-flops sank into the grass and icy cold water ran along my feet, jarring in the hot night air. "What?" My voice startled me. I went closer, but it was just Death, still as plastic, standing there. I turned around to see if the lawn was underwater but the water, despite being up to my ankles and cold, stopped before it got to the sidewalk. I crouched to touch the stream and it disappeared. Only grass was there. I stood again and the water flowed. Our tiny patch of grass was made of river. "What even?"

There was movement behind me, so I turned to look at Death. Those black pits of eyes were suddenly an inch from my face. His voice was deep and terrible, his face real with bone, his eyes black pits, as he said, "Don't forget your costume."

I woke up with a start in my bed. That wasn't a dream, I knew it in my gut. Dreams feel different. I just wasn't sure how the night had ended. Death had moved and scared the shit out of me. Death said, "Don't forget your costume." As if. I rubbed my face and checked the clock. It was still dark out, but it was 6:45. Time to get my shit together for school.

Only when I got to the door of my room did I notice my flip-flops sitting in the corner. Their foam-padded soles were soaking wet.

Dad let me have the car that Friday to pick up the costume. Weather never could make up its mind for Halloween. We'd had drizzly Halloweens, and hot blowy Halloweens. The trick was to make your costume adjustable. Layers underneath for cold nights, but the ability to be pared down in case of trick or treating in 80-degree heat. I was a bit worried by the 80 degrees today and my wool nineteenth-century costume, because damn it, it was perfect, and losing even the waistcoat or the jacket would ruin the whole effect. Plus, add a mask and it was gonna be stifling.

When I got to *Halloween Beyond*, the place was packed. People in for last-minute vampire blood, picking up costumes, returning things. The moment I opened the front door, I realized it was going to be a bit of a wait in a space where social distance was an impossibility.

I put on my N95 and squished my way past the rows of last-minute costume shoppers, through the sexy pirate crowd, and sidled up to the back glass counter by the tree and that gaping maw of a door. The counter was surprisingly uncrowded, only one other person there.

Maeve came out from behind the curtain laden down with a box and two costumes draped over the top of it. Her hair was in a bun with a pencil stuck through it, her expression a bit frazzled as she held her hand up to the guy, *one minute* and disappeared behind the curtain again. When she came back through, she saw me and winked. The guy was taking long enough to buy the shop itself, but I waited as she dealt with him, and I focused on the bloody knife options in the display case. Another Halloween I'd definitely pick one of these up. I wasn't sure what Halloween was like in college, but I imagined a lot of Solo cups, beer pong, and half-assed costumes.

"Here you go." The closeness of Maeve's voice startled me. She was right in front of me with my costume. I had remembered it more frayed, but it looked like it was brand new from a shop in the 19th century. She slipped the top hat out of its bag. "Do you know how to open this?"

I imagined you'd push the top up and pull the brim away, but that wasn't knowing. I shook my head.

She grinned and whacked the brim on her forearm, and the hat sprang to full size. Very cool. "And to compact it again, a flat surface, careful of the fabric." She pressed it down in the center with the palm of her hand. It was maybe the coolest thing I'd ever seen.

"Thank you, thank you so much, it looks amazing." My voice squeaked. What an ass.

"So, Lex . . . " I was stunned she remembered my name. "Halloween night, gonna be amazing." She patted the suit significantly. Not sure what that meant. "Round about midnight tho, I'm gonna need a favor for a friend."

"Oh, shit, is this about drugs or something? Because I'm . . . " People sometimes mistook my tailored clothing choices, the purple dye in my short-cropped hair for me being part of Duncan's crowd. That I was not.

Her laugh made me sorry I'd said it. "I promise it's nothing like that. Just. Um. You'll see, let's touch base at midnight."

"I can't get away." How would I explain taking the car out at midnight?

"At your place."

"Okaaay. How do you . . . ?"

She interrupted, "You will have more adventures in life if you don't play it safe. Asking that is playing it safe."

Her green eyes burned with an extra intensity for a moment and something in me said, "*Okay*."

She said, "See you soon."

I took the costume and shoved my way through the crowd. There wasn't much air in this place, and I didn't have time in my life to get sick. When I pushed out the front door and made my way to the car, I noticed the temperature had dropped by like ten degrees. The wind was changing to onshore. By the time I got home a thick fog had settled and the setting sun had turned the orange world a Novembery purple. The suit wouldn't be too hot! It was a perfect night for Halloween.

I rushed to my room and put the suit on. It fit surprisingly well. I'd always found I was too long and too skinny for things to fit right, but the shirt, the vest, the trousers all fit like they'd been tailored for me. I fastened the black leather belt which had a worn silver buckle. Put on the velvet waistcoat and buttoned it. A filigreed silver chain hung from the side pocket, and I reached inside, pulling out a heavy solid silver pocket watch. Something led me to click on the button at the side and the face sprang open. I checked the time on my phone and adjusted the watch, closing it with a satisfying *snick*. I held the watch to my ear and held my breath, the ticking was grounding somehow. A sound I recognized from another time, perhaps. Maybe as a kid? I put on the black wool jacket with its two silver buttons at the waist and an ever so slight gathering at the back that suggested tails. The jacket flowed with a familiar flourish. I pulled the top hat out of its bag and stood in front of the mirror, one eyebrow arched, and tried like hell to look as cool as Maeve when I whacked it on my forearm. It sprang open with a fabric rustle and flutter. It was lined in red and a sewn-in label at its very bottom read, in an antique font, *Halloween Beyond.*

As I doffed my hat, I said, "Beyond indeed." I smoothed out the jacket and felt something in the right pocket. I reached in and pulled it out. A brand-new forest green N-95 mask just like Maeve's. I had to laugh.

I wore the suit downstairs and Mom said, "Damn, Lex you look phenomenal!" I did a twirl for her, and . . . were those tears? She said, "Honey, I'm so proud of you. You . . . " She paused and I was worried she would go into a total bawling like she had at my eighth-grade graduation, but she pulled herself together and said, "Lex, you've always been a hundred percent yourself."

Hit me right in the chest with a warm overflow which made things hella awkward. I said, "Thanks, Mom," trying to keep my voice from cracking and I skirted past her to the front yard where Dad was setting up the lights for the night. The fog was thick now, such the opposite of this crackling dry morning, but it meant for a good trick or treat night.

Dad was crouched in front of Death.

"Um, Dad . . . "

He looked up and saw me and something came over him and he rose to his feet, his eyes softening. "Lex, you look amazing."

"Thanks, Dad." I stepped between the tentacles of electrical wires running from the animatronics to a power strip.

He said, "That's so you. I just." The tears, what was it with the tears?

I said, "Can I do anything?" Anything, make this stop.

"Yeah, can you stay here while I plug it in, tell me it's working?"

I nodded, hopscotched through the cords to get to the light. I was feeling good, I'd finished filling out the application, my essays could wait. I could forget them for one night anyway. My homework was done for the week, and I felt like it was the first time I'd breathed in a while. I had totally forgotten for a moment about the night before.

I stood next to Death and got an echo of a funny feeling, the water on my feet, the stream. I looked up at him, frozen in his plastic face. I thought about what Maeve had said.

There was no water right now, but the lap of water echoed just beyond sound's reach.

Dad's yell came from around the house, "Is it on?"

I looked down and the light he'd set up was there on its black stand, completely under water. I had an impulse to jump, water, electrical cords and all, but the cords were gone.

"Lex! Is it on?"

I looked back at him and back at the grass, dry, tangled with cords again. My knees were lit up with a blue-gelled light. "Yep!"

Dad was next to me in an instant. "Good. We don't have to go to the store again." He put his arm around my shoulder and squeezed me to him. I realized we were the same height now. I was feeling all kinds of ways today.

The family friends we'd spent every Halloween with—with the obvious absence of Duncan and his mom—came over at five. Bella and Josie came, of course. Some friends of Maria and Mike. It was a crazy raucous noisy group, hanging out for photos, noshing on black bean soup and fingers in a blanket, the parents cracking into the beer and wine and getting louder as they drank.

Dad was already at work out front, stuffing a bucket with rolls of toilet paper soaked in sterno for the giant jack o'lantern. He had carved it out of a hundred-and-fifty-pound pumpkin the night before. He'd light it only when it got dark and when he did, one roll of TP at a time, what a terror. Flames at least three feet tall brought the jack o'lantern's terrifying expression to life. He'd had everyone from passersby to the fire department worried about a fire spreading, but it hadn't yet, and nothing gave him greater glee than being scolded by a concerned neighbor. Luck of the holiday, bad things never happened to the King of Halloween.

Mike and his buds snuck off to his room to play video games until trick or treating. Maria and her friends hung on the lawn alternating between handing out candy and trying to scare the bigger kids. Maria was a ghost bride this year, so it was easy. Something about her makeup and her tiny size was eerie to begin with. But when she sat stock still among the statuary and animatronics in the front yard, she got lost among the various figures. When she *did* move and people looked a little harder at her, they'd jump and yelp. Something alive in the midst of these animatronic figures was more terrifying even than a Jack-in-the-box clown. And the addition of an N-95 made it even creepier.

It was so nice to have the gang back together, I thought Dad's heart would break in the quarantine last year, the first Halloween in his whole life we just couldn't. It was more important to keep the kids safe.

No Duncan tonight, of course. I don't know why he was on my mind so much today. I always dwelled on him on Halloween, but this year was kinda extra. I guess it was because this was my last childhood Halloween. I guess it was part of feeling all kinds of ways.

It wasn't quite dark yet. We waited on the front lawn where the grownups were already in their cups, drinking, handing out candy to the ittybitties whose parents wanted them to trick or treat before things got dark and wild. The kids were so cute. Most of the costumes were homemade around here. One kid had a metal framework covered with gauze lit up with colored twinkle lights. He made a fantastic jellyfish, and the effect would get better as the night went on. Another tiny kid was dressed as Grogu—green face fake ears—with his dad Mandalorian. In Glendale, Halloween was a high holy day and all the geeks who worked for Dreamworks and Disney were in their element, going overboard on their front lawns and kids' costumes.

I was happy to revel in it, to let go of all that stress for one night, and once again embrace the holiday. This was a joyful return. This was family and these family friends were so chill and those of us who were seniors could let go of the psycho pressures put on us this fall: SATs, colleges, where we might go, if we qualified for work study, had we done enough volunteer hours, and what stupid major we were going to take. Instead, we reminisced about our Halloween adventures of yore. Bella, Josie, and I laughed and shuddered about the time that creepy old guy tried to talk us into his house when we were in fifth grade. It was the first time we were allowed out to trick or treat without parents. Bella said, "Thank God, Lex stood tough."

Josie said to Bella. "Not like you, you were like, 'Hey he says there's candy in there. Let's go with this guy into his creepy house.'"

Bella said, "Anything for candy."

Josie said, "Murder or child slavery."

Bella said, "I think he just wanted some friends."

We howled with laughter. These two always had my back no matter the stage of my life. We went back to third grade when our parents met at a PTO meeting where all the parents were losing their minds over something or another. Not our Moms. They were in the back and snuck out after for drinks. Luckily Josie, Bella, and I were already friends. There was probably a reason for that.

"Sooooo . . . " I said as we lay on my bed staring at the ceiling as we had so many Halloweens past. "We trick or treating tonight?"

Josie, who had gone low maintenance with cat ears, a black outfit, and an adorable triangle nose and whiskers of black paint on her mask, looked at me sideways. "We're a little old for that, yeah?"

I said, "Last ride. C'mon."

Bella groaned, "Let's go visit that house that almost kidnapped us."

"Eww . . . gross," said Josie.

"I'll bring the eggs," I said. We heaved off the bed, Bella's jaguar Onesie tail got caught under my butt, so it took a few tries, but we grabbed a finger in a blanket each and made our way out the door into the misty night, which had finally turned dark. We just wanted to be out and kids again one last time.

"Your time has come. Two coins and your passage is secured." Death's tinny recorded voice hit us as we stepped out. "Get into the boat."

I squinted up at him sideways when Josie skipped to the street. She said, "C'mon! It's getting late!"

Bella tugged my sleeve. "Let's go get 'em."

Death said, "I'll see you at midnight." Only it wasn't his recorded voice. It was a real voice. *His real voice?* The one I'd heard the night before. I swung to look up into his plastic face once more, but it looked real. Dad's lights were really good. I lifted up my hand, carefully, toward his brooding skull. Plastic. I rubbed down his cheekbone and it was bone, cold and solid and real. My hand went up and it was plastic again.

"Leeeeeeeeexxxxxxxxxxxxxxxxxx." They were in chorus, and I was clearly losing my mind. Sleep deprivation. Stress. Whatever it was, it was time to get out of here.

As I headed toward them, Josie said, "Don't get all creepy on Death, babe. He's not that into you."

Bella punched her arm and said, "Death's nonbinary you nimrod. They." She turned to me the laugh already in her eyes, "They are just not that into you."

I made an effort to laugh to look normal. So they wouldn't see what I realized. That this was all something, the wet flip-flops, the bony face, the growing sense of excitement tinged with fear. That creeping of dread in the bottom of my stomach. This wasn't nothing.

We started up toward the main drag, Kenneth Road. The ittybitties and their parents were sticking to the side streets. Kenneth ran through the heart of the neighborhood and was lined with enormous houses known for giving out full-sized candy bars. Halloween night, it was mostly for teenagers, passing in mad crushing packs. I couldn't help but grin like a fool at the hominess of it all. We were back in action after the quarantine just last year when no one was out, when my dad, the King of Halloween sat in a chair forlorn as Mom tried to substitute all this joy with movies and candy and hot apple cider. Even the fingers in a blanket didn't taste right that year.

But look at us now! I loved this neighborhood. I loved these girls who'd been with me through thick and thin. Who stood up to my bullies in third grade through junior high. And back at it again after last year was stolen by COVID, this, *this* was our night. *Forget Duncan, it's his own fault he's missing it.*

We passed Mike on the street. Rather, my pigeon brother and his unicorn, horse, and cardinal friends. All of them wore men's suits, complete with ties. It was kinda priceless, with rubber masks molded into the heads of those animals. They were so much cooler than they even knew they were. I jumped in front of them and yelled, "Stop, fools!"

Pigeon head came off first. Mike was looking at me funny, kinda in awe. "You look amazing, Lex, wow."

The cardinal head came off and it was Jorge, not Armen as I'd thought. He said, "Hey, Lex. Good to see you. Last time out, huh?" Thing is, Jorge hadn't talked to me in four years since I became Lex and when forced to, he tried not to use my name. He was one of the guys who had trouble with me, but here he was seeing me full on.

Horsehead followed. Oh, that was Armen. "Hey Lex!"

Then Unicorn. That of course was James. Sheepish, "Hey, Lex."

My brother's friends who'd ignored me before had stopped full stop on Halloween night among all their hijinks to say hello.

It was weird.

I said, "Hi, guys. Okay, well, we're headed out."

They all murmured together. "Bye Lex."

"See you, Lex."

"I'll be over next week!" hollered Armen. A burst of laughter from his friends and they shoved him around after that.

One of them mocked Armen, "I'll be over next week!"

I felt like I was suddenly famous or something.

Bella and Josie came in on either side of me and took my arm. Josie said, "Oh my God, what even was that?"

Bella mimicked, "Byyeee, Lex."

"Weird." I knew it was the suit. There was something about this suit and Maeve who gave it to me. I had never felt more comfortable in my own skin. Mom and Dad saw it. Bella and Josie who had always, always, seen me no matter what was up with my name or pronouns, maybe they didn't. They'd both said I looked good, but . . .

"Lex!" Jason from *Friday the Thirteenth* stood in my path.

"Hello?" Halloween was the one night serial killers didn't scare me.

He lifted his mask, it was Duncan, and my heart rushed in happiness at seeing him, at his speaking to me, until I saw that he was totally amped up on something or other. He said, "Halloween night. Your house looks GREAT!"

"Thank you!" We were yelling to be heard above the crowd.

"That new addition, Death? It looks like he's coming right for you!" Duncan's pupils were pinpoints even in the dark, his blue eyes fully blue, his face flushed. He stared at me for a curiously long moment and wavered a little toward me. Part of me worried he'd fall on me.

I said, "You okay, Duncan?"

"I'm so very glad to see you. I. I just wanted to say I'm sorry."

"For what?" I knew for what, but I wasn't going to let him have it easy.

His focus lasered into me and he stared for an uncomfortable moment. He looked at the ground and said, "I miss you."

God this was weird. I mean he was SO fucked up, I could just pin it on that.

Bella grabbed my arm and leaned in toward him, "Some fucking nerve, Duncan. Save your apology for a sober day." She had a knack for saying exactly what needed to be said.

Josie said, "Nice to see you, Duncan. Take care of yourself tonight."

I let myself be led away by Bella, but looked over my shoulder and watched Duncan standing in the crowd, swaying, a bit lost. I had a very deep urge to go fetch him and bring him home, let Mom get some water into him, maybe some soup, but Michael Myers and Ghostface from Scream stepped up next to him. My guess was Charlie was Ghostface, no sad backstory on that guy, he was pure evil. They guided Duncan off into the night . . . to party harder, I imagined. His totally drugged out gone-ness made his absence I'd been stewing over that week even more real. I refused to cry one more tear for that wasteoid.

We walked through the crammed sidewalks and up the path to Mrs. Schweitzer's house where we knew she'd be happy to see us even though we were big. She was always good for full bars. Her house was right on Kenneth and had a long diagonal sidewalk, which was at present packed with groups of large trick or treaters, crammed in, and shoving to get past each other. In the midst of all these big kids was a group of littles, a Dorothy, a Fireman, and a little JayJay the Jetplane, who wore the cutest sweatshirt with a little red light pinned to his navy-blue hoodie. His mom had made him blue Styrofoam wings that hung off the sweatshirt. It was adorable and they were behind a group of teenagers at the door of the house. In the scramble on the front porch, the big kids mushed past the littles to get off and I heard a *snap*. Both JayJay's wings had broken off.

Josie stooped to grab them and pick them up. "Oh no, little guy!"

The kid's face was crumpling, and he was welling up with tears.

His mom stepped in real quick. "Don't worry, don't worry. Nothing a little duct tape won't fix. Thank you. Thank you for being good kids." She smiled at Josie and when she saw me, her face lit up. Only then did I recognize her.

"Mrs. Lazar!" Our sixth-grade teacher. I said, "Guys, it's Mrs. Lazar!"

She said, "Lex. Lex look at you, all grown up, I can't believe it."

I have no idea how she knew my proper name. But this town was small. She was so focused on me, that I felt bad for Josie and Bella. I prompted, "And Josie Reyes and Bella Narvaez."

She looked at them and squinted, thinking a moment. I was getting kind of pissed at her for forgetting because Bella looked EXACTLY like her second-grade self only grown up and pretty and Josie hadn't changed at all. But I guess with masks it's harder. Mrs. Lazar said, "Of course! How are you all doing?" She didn't remember them. She knew me though. "Lex, it's good to see you. You about ready for college now, right?"

"Yeah."

"Great! That doesn't surprise me at all. You'll do good things, kid, I have a good feeling about it." It was kind of creepy the intensity with which she was regarding me like she saw right through me. She sensed the awkwardness and broke it, "I've got to go repair JayJay, but it does my heart good to see you're doing well."

I was still looking back at JayJay holding his sad wings and Mrs. Lazar when Mrs. Schweitzer opened the front door. "Ahhh! My favorite neighborhood monsters, all grown up!"

"Happy Halloween!"

It was the first time Halloween was on a weekend since we were little, so of course, Bella and Josie had to sleep over. We were soooo tired and candy drunk, but for one night we had taken a break, and that was so nice. We put on *The Omen* and sang along with the spooky soundtrack until we ran out of steam and passed out.

My ten-minute appointment alarm on my phone woke me up. It was almost midnight. Maria was bunking in with Mom, but Rachel and Bella's snores were just as homey as hers. Maybe a college roommate wouldn't be so bad after all.

Midnight. What the hell was this supposed to be anyway? Some chick I'd met at the costume store said to meet her at midnight. Death had said or I *imagined* Death had said "See you at midnight." This was nuts.

But that feeling, that anticipation tickled once again. I sat upright. Well, I was thirsty *and* I had to pee, what would it hurt me to at least investigate? After the bathroom, I padded into the kitchen, got a drink of water. I'd slept in my costume, and I didn't know why waking up wasn't more uncomfortable. Those hotdogs from the fingers in a blanket were salty, so I poured a second glass of water, slipped into my boots, and stepped out front of the house to sit. Death was as still as the rest of the animatronics and without Dad's music or the chorus of the creatures' recordings and their laughter and creepy sayings, the street was quieter than it had been that night. There was some stray noise coming down from Kenneth, a few whoops and hollers. A random siren here or there as the cops pulled over drunk drivers.

This was a good Halloween. I was glad for all of it even this moment to sit quietly remembering, as I sat on the porch waiting for God knows what. I loved the suit that suited me, that Halloween was back, I loved the old friends we'd seen, a last hurrah. Running into Duncan was weird. I'd told myself over and over these past five years that worrying about him was fruitless, but still, I worried. He was in a bad way. I should check up on him, but it's not like I had his cell number since he blocked me, and calling his mom would be just weird, especially since that's what started our rift.

He blocked me sophomore year. After I'd seen him in the gym, so totally wasted, I reached out to his mom that I was worried. She had always been my second mom. Said I thought he was using drugs. She had to know that already, everyone did.

She said, "Oh. Thank you. Oh god, I. Thank you for telling me. We've been trying to find his father and it's been a lot for him."

"He's *missing*?"

She sighed, long and impatient. "No, not exactly. He's just. Don't worry about it. Grownup stuff. Just, Lex, thank you again. You should know you did the right thing." And right as I hung up, I knew I hadn't. I don't know what happened after that, I only know the next day Duncan blocked me on his phone and on all his social media. A week later I found a postcard in my locker. It was a Harry Potter postcard which was a burn because that was our favorite shared obsession for three years there. It read, "Stay out of my life, Potter." He signed it Draco.

Getting over Duncan wasn't just one step. Getting over Duncan was going to take me a lifetime. I burned that card in a fit a few weeks after getting it.

I looked up at the night sky which in true fog form was orange with light pollution.

A light caught my eye and I looked down the street where someone in a shimmering robe was making their way toward me. When I say shimmer, you'd think I mean glittery or lit up like that wonderful jellyfish costume I'd seen earlier. Nope. The fabric on this costume glowed from within and rippled like it was made of liquid moonlight.

The costume crossed the street toward me, and I hoped to catch a glimpse of what made it so *alive*. When she started up our front walk to the house and lowered her hood, I saw that it was Maeve, only more so. Her hair was most definitely not stuck up with a pencil. It cascaded around her shoulders, entwined with living things made of light and greenery and branches. Without a mask she was more stunning, a nose strong enough to hold her enormous eyes, a wry mouth, and a mischievously pointed chin . . . Her skin, luminous in the Halloween store, now glowed with energy that crackled outward and through her hair? Or was that a trick of the night? Her cloak rippled and shimmered. Her smile was the same though when she saw me. She said, "You had a good night."

I said, "I had a very good night."

"I wanted you to know what it felt like to be seen for exactly who you are."

Of course, it was the suit. "It was weird."

"But you're feeling yourself now, aren't you?"

I nodded. "I don't understand, I picked that costume myself."

Maeve said, "We don't have time. Three minutes."

She motioned me over to her. The liquid cape was, leaking? Flowing? I said, "What is that cape even made of? It's a total trip."

She shushed me silently and knelt, the cape a puddle, at the edge of the lawn where our burned out jack o' lanterns and candy wrappers littered the patch of grass in front of Death's boat. As we knelt close, I breathed in; she smelled like earth, things growing, in the kind of way that reaches out to you on a transformative spring day . . . the kind that seeps through your sneakers and makes you run and jump for no reason at all. She smelled like life, the chaparral after a rain, the world gone green.

She said, "I need a favor for my friend here. I promised him."

She ran her fingers through the grass and stopped, murmuring under her breath. The grass turned to water, deeper this time, and the jack o'lanterns bobbed in surprise until they caught water and sank. The few uncarved pumpkins floated around Death's boat. There was a creaking noise, water flowing, and I noticed Death's robes changing first. That cheap Halloween cloth gave way to a heavily hooded cloak, the gray plastic of his face filled in with genuine bone. The dark patches painted in were real holes in a very real skull like I'd seen earlier that night. Death turned his head and looked right at me. He then turned to Maeve and damn if his jaw didn't drop a little. Maeve smiled and patted her side, which seemed an odd thing to do with a seven-foot version of Death. I looked back at him for his reaction, which was to step out of the boat and go to her. He turned and handed me his oar. For that's what it was, in its real form. I took it hesitantly.

"What am I supposed to do with this?"

Death shrugged and said, "You know, make sure they pay their coins. Let them talk. Just get them to the other side."

The other side of where? But the moment I took that oar everything shifted anyway. I wasn't on my front sidewalk anymore. I was standing on the banks of a river, in some sort of enormous cave or space. A cave with no ceiling? My eyes followed the walls up into blackness and I looked above me into its void, thick and silent. My stomach sank in terror. My idea of the worst . . . that blackness. I looked back down to the dark gray black sand beneath my feet and scuffed my boots a little to remind myself I was in a place. I breathed. Maeve, in this environment, shone like the moon and her cape rippled in the blackness like it was part of it, crackling with the energy of everything around her. She said, "We won't be long. You'll hold the fort, right?"

"Hold the fort. Okay." My voice echoed in the cavern.

She walked a few steps toward me with those green magical eyes set. As much as I'd felt seen in my suit, I was completely seen in this moment. She said, "You have a friend who needs you. Take the coins, get them across, we'll be back soon."

She turned. The tall, black-cloaked figure and the small one fell into step and within ten steps Death had turned into an enormous black dog at her side, and they were off down my street, down the beach, and then my street was gone, and it was only me and the boat and the cavern and the water.

I looked around, uncertain what to do. Finally, I just got in the boat and sat. I have no idea why I didn't panic, again, I am never okay with blackness. Maybe the suit, maybe Maeve just had a way. For the first time in a while, I felt like I was somewhere I was supposed to be. The boat rocked a little, the water lapping its edges. In front of me in the center of the cliff of dark rock was a darker archway. I assumed people came through here. I wonder what you'd feel coming through, seeing Death waiting on a boat. I guess you'd kind of know. I wonder if it was disappointing. Or terrifying for people who died suddenly. I both wanted no one to come while they were gone, and kind of wanted someone to come while they were gone. The oar lay across my lap, and I stretched to crack my back, but it wouldn't. The scraped knee I'd gotten getting the shit out of the attic didn't hurt. What's crazy was it was what, at least 12:30? I wasn't tired. Time and space here was simply . . . correct. I could feel things I touched, and the smell of water and stone was unmistakable. I saw clearly as far as the light would allow, but it was just. Still? Crystalline?

Something white came out of the tunnel toward me. I stood up and took Death's position, holding the paddle just so. I tried to look dignified. This was an important job. The white figure turned out to be an old woman in a hospital gown. She was tiny, 5 feet at the most, and her short white hair floated around her head like it was under water. Gravity-defying or just bed-head it was hard to tell. Her movements were spry though, she slowed when she saw me. I reached for a mask but realized how absurd that was. Of course, I didn't have one and this was . . . well COVID didn't seem relevant here.

"Well, you're not what I was expecting at all." There was something in her frankness I really liked. She looked up and around her, squinting into the dark above her.

I made my voice as deep and steady as I could, "That'll be two coins please." What kind of coins? Quarters?

She mimed reaching around for her wallet, a sparkle in her green eyes.

I laughed. But then actual amazement crossed her face as her outfit morphed entirely. Blue jeans, white collar shirt, bright red v-neck sweater. Decent boots. She reached into her newfound pocket and pulled out two gold coins, saying, "Huh." About her clothes, she said, "Well, that's more like it." Her hair was browner, there were fewer lines on her face. She smiled and handed me the coins. "I guess these are for you." She laughed.

I took them, not quite sure what to do with them, but once they hit my palm they disappeared and the boat swayed a bit, ready to go. "Get in, I guess." Damn, lost all authority.

She smiled at me and said, "You're new here, huh?"

"Yeah."

"Me too." She sat and looked into the distance. I only had to touch the oar to the water and the boat took off, steady and slow. The woman sat and didn't speak for a moment. Then she said, "This wasn't what I expected."

I said, "Me neither."

"I mean, pearly gates maybe. Or iron ones if I was *really* bad." She said this in a tone of amusement. "The river. The boat driven by a . . . " That pause was usually deadly for me, but she said, "A teenager. You are a teenager, right?"

"Yeah. For another year at least."

She laughed. "Wouldn't wish more than that on you. You just seem really young for this job." She fell silent.

After a time, I said, "You okay?"

"Well . . . " She waggled her head back and forth, the way Maria used to when she was six. "I imagine so. Pretty decent life all in all. Good friends. A few years I coulda done without. But I guess that's everyone."

"I guess so." I didn't want to think about bad years. Aside from a few bumps, things had been pretty sweet so far.

There was a forever element to this journey and a sudden element as the boat hit the shore on the opposite side. No pearly gates. Just another tunnel. At the end of this tunnel though, there was light glowing, growing in strength. That gave me a little hope.

I said, "So, any advice?"

She chuckled long and low. "I don't know kid. Be good to your friends. Don't stress too much about the career stuff. If you keep working the right thing will happen. If you want to go to grad school, wait a few years and see if you really have to. Oh." She got up and stepped out of the boat to face me. "Always look for the funny people. They'll keep you going when things get weird."

"Thanks." It wasn't everything really. They weren't really the kind of answers I was looking for. But it seemed like decent advice.

She turned and walked into the tunnel in the rock which flashed with light and the sounds of a crowded cocktail party, people laughing and talking. She walked into it, saying, "Well, hello! So great to see you all!"

It went dark and she was gone. I wondered what I was supposed to do. Row across again, I imagine. A part of me wanted to peek further down the tunnel, but I knew better than to tempt death. Before I could manage to turn around, I had somehow been transported back to the first tunnel and was waiting again. The boat knew the way, I guess.

DEATH

Danu is shifty that way. It has been so long since I've last seen her, I didn't recognize her at first. She is like the memory of knowing someone. Maeve. Really only the name had changed.

Over the years, she would check in on me from time to time, but those times were so many crossings apart . . . I lost track. I always enjoyed her company tremendously. I'm a funny guy, that's one thing most folks don't get. They're so obsessed with the fact that they're gone, and I'm supposed to be all somber and give them space to make the passage and everything, it's just not the right space for jokes. I tried once. A comedian had died, a guy who made no small fortune off making people laugh. Turns out he had no sense of humor whatsoever. It was very disappointing.

It's nice to have her back for a moment. And it feels good to be a dog again, my body liquid and so mobile, flexible. My pads relish each texture, grass, sidewalk, street, water. My nose picks up every delicious smell this plane has to offer. Tonight, the smells are thick with sugar, kids, smoke machines, and something burning. There's a hot dog someone dropped, yum. A candy bar.

Danu laughs. Her laughter makes me want to run in circles around her, leap in the air. "I expect it's late enough, go ahead, run!"

And I'm off, drinking up the air in large, delicious gulps, the sounds of my pads hitting the ground, leaping over anything that gets in my way. When I get far enough, I cycle back and run to

Danu. And then another circle. I do this about six times before I fall into step with her again. We walk and the night gets mistier, and the smells change completely. The mist is thicker, and smells of ocean, damp laurel, and heather. A peat fire burning. There are no sidewalks now, only grass and dirt and bracken and we are walking up a hill toward a small building with a light on. As we get closer something in me recognizes it. I stop in my tracks and sit.

Danu turns to me. "It's time to make this right now."

It hurts too much to see, a very human sob escapes me, and I look down at my hands, no longer paws, are covered with flesh for the first time in an age. I haven't always been on that river you see. Onetime, in the before, I had a life.

Danu says, "One night."

But centuries have passed.

She says, "She's waiting for you. Go make it right."

LEX

Next was a really little kid. Just five. Made me want to cry just to see her, dirty overalls, baffled look on her face. But when she saw me, she smiled and reached out her hand. I took her hand and helped her in the boat. I didn't want to know what had killed her, so I didn't ask the questions burning me.

All I said was, "Are you scared?"

She shook her head. She bobbed in her seat like she was excited. "Wow this cave is really *big*."

"Yep, it is."

We got to the other side with no more talking. This tiny person's little overalls had gone clean on the journey. With her hair tied up in perfect yellow plastic baubles, she stepped toward the doorway without a backward glance.

The light flashed bright, and a woman came out. The girl ran to her and jumped into her arms and they both made a cry like coming home. The woman looked back at me, cocked her head curiously, and mouthed "Thank you." And took her baby to the other side.

Of course, I cried. Who do you think I am?

DEATH

The wind is chill and whips against my cape and a shiver runs up my sides. My sides are flesh. How can I feel this in my present form? I look down at my hands again and they are thick with red hairs on my fingers. They are familiar and this frightens me. I do not know why I am here, but I know with a marrow-deep certainty that I do not want to be here.

I turn to Danu, whose cloak is now ordinary broadcloth. She is dressed in the clothing of the time, my time. I say, "What is this?"

"It's time you remember what you did. Why you have been Death for nearly a millennium. It's time for a reckoning."

Give me my boat back. My simple task. My job. My purpose. Give it back. This is a bad place. I can't be here.

As if in answer she says, "I'll leave you here. You have the night."

I walk toward that low stone house I'd laid myself one backbreaking summer. Plough the field, hit a rock, add it to the house. I look up at the roof whose thatching I hadn't kept up with and I know inside is the wife I have no right to claim.

I open the door and the warmth and the home smells from inside—damp thatch, wool, wood fire, soup on the stove, and the smell of my wife prick my eyes.

"Callum," she says. And in that naming, laden with sorrow and pain, my memories and my life come back to me. I have already done the most evil thing that cannot be made right.

LEX

He was blinking in the light and for a moment I was happy to see it was him, and he looked present and *clean*, like the Duncan I knew before. It was like my old friend had come to visit me in this lonely place.

Then I remembered what this meant. "No." *Nonononono. Not Duncan. Not yet.*

"Lex?" he tilted his head and gazed directly up into the blackness and then back at me and his face grimaced in fear like when we were seven and he thought my pile of clothes was a monster.

Let them talk. Get them across.

I said, "Are you . . . did you . . . " I stopped myself. It was traitorous to think of it, so I simply asked, "What's the last thing you remember?"

He thought a moment, and said, "I was on Charlie's front lawn. They were all yelling and worried. Someone was pressing on my chest, it felt . . . heavy."

Not on purpose. At least he didn't do this to himself.

I remembered what I'd been charged with and what Maeve had said. Although I didn't know how I would be *helping* him, exactly. Seems like Death could have done it just the same.

Duncan said, "I don't think I'm supposed to be here."

"What did you take?"

"I. It was just a few edibles. But then Charlie had these pills. The capsules we've been selling. Well, it must have been those."

Selling? Great, he was dealing now. "How many did you take?" *Idiot.* Our school had announced reports of pills hitting the neighborhoods laced with heroin and worse.

He lowered his eyes and mumbled, "I don't remember."

"Damn, dude. I. I wanted you to hit rock bottom, see the error of your ways, get clean. I didn't want . . . " I trailed off.

Listen. Help them to the other side.

He welled up with tears. He said, "I didn't want this. Oh God, what's my mom gonna do? Shit."

I lay the oar across the boat and went to him and threw my arms around him hugging him hard. I wasn't going to. I wasn't going to. Goddamn it, I was crying. He didn't return the hug for a moment, and then his arms went up to my back and he hugged back. "Aw, shit, Lex, I'm sorry."

He smelled like Duncan, like home. I said, "No, don't. I shoulda. I shoulda fought harder. I shoulda. Like an intervention or something. I shoulda got my parents involved. We could have . . . "

"Stop. Stop." One last squeeze and he stepped back. He stood there and I could tell he was like, not saying a million things because I knew him, only I didn't know what they were because I didn't know him anymore. Finally, after a long pause, he said, "So, what's next?"

I imitated the animatronic, "Two coins to pass. Get in the boat." I ran over and got the oar and took my position.

Duncan said, "How'd you land this job? I mean, you're the right person for it with the hugs and you always care about people, but . . . "

"It's just for the night. Maeve said . . . Death needed. Aw hell, I don't know exactly, but here we are."

He was suddenly afraid again. He said, "Are you?" He drew his finger across his neck.

"No. No. I don't think so, at least. She said they'd see me in the morning."

He said, "This is weird."

I said, "That's what a lot of people say." I was the expert all of a sudden, after transporting two souls.

He climbed into the boat. His hair wasn't dyed anymore, it was the dirty brown it always was. He wasn't wearing his Jason costume, but his standard school outfit, rocker t-shirt, worn-out jacket, and the Sharpie illustrated Converse I'd seen him wear since we were small. I got the feeling souls appeared in the outfits that were most *them*. I wondered if, when my time came, I'd appear in this suit.

He sat in front of me, and I gasped audibly.

He said, "What?"

"Nothing."

I wasn't prepared to see that pink Africa-shaped birthmark at the back of his neck, nor the way it made me feel. Duncan, man. There's a lot we never talked about. I had so many questions.

I pushed off from shore. The trip was quiet and seemed longer than the others. I wondered if it was as long as each person needed.

I said, "How's your mom?"

"Well, she's not gonna be so great now, is she?"

Shit. I didn't answer. *Listen.*

He swore under his breath and said, "We were just getting a handle on where my Dad was . . . "

"You what? Didn't you know he'd gone to Florida?"

Duncan looked up into the black void and roared an *aaaarghhh!* "Florida, then Missouri, then the Caymans and that's when the trouble started."

"I didn't know. Any of this, I'm so sorry."

"Not like you would." There wasn't bitterness in his voice, only surrender.

"Not like you'd tell me anything." There was some bitterness in mine.

He breathed in long before he said, "I was embarrassed, okay? Mom was embarrassed and didn't want your mom to know. He took everything, the savings, my college fund, the house."

"I knew about the house," I muttered this, and it felt useless against everything he was going through, everything I hadn't been there for.

"He took *her* savings she'd been working to save up for my college before I was even born. She worked on movie sets, you know, had a good salary."

"That's how she met your dad." Pulling up a file from when we used to share everything only brought to light how much I didn't know Duncan now.

"That's how she met my dad. And now we can't find him to even extradite this, and we can't afford the forensic accountants to figure it all out. I'd just gotten a job at the Home Depot, we were saving up again, now what is she going to do?"

DEATH

She had chosen the name Maureen because her own name was unpronounceable. I was a fool for laying my trap, a fool for thinking entrapping her would be the same as possessing her. That any of that would be anything like love. Most of all, I was simply a fool.

But let me take it back to the beginning, for context.

I was said to be a handsome lad, tall, red-haired, strong-faced, but not brawny or built. I did enough farm work I should have been, but I couldn't lose that lankiness, the concave chested frame of my dad. Either way, I had my pick of girls in the town. I sometimes abused their good will, but lived a carefree life with my Dadaigh in our little cottage near the sea with a small stretch of farmland and a view of the ocean. I imagine that's how I'd gotten so foolish. Mam had died having me, so there was no wisdom and Dad was not a man of many words. Having only lived with my mother a scant year, he hardly had the knowledge or tools to tell me how to be with women. He did say, and I'm not saying I blame him here, but he did say, "Once you catch her, m'boy, dinna let her go."

Whatever my reason, it was very bad judgment. I was only twenty when I first saw her. I've met enough people since then to know that at 20, as a lad, you're not using your whole head. At 20, you're certain you know everything, what is best, that your parents are fools and that you're better off on your own than tied up in any one place. Particularly in town. I'd been sweet on Aisling from down the lane for a few years, but then I didn't pay her enough attention, and Farlan from town had *his* shoulders grow in, that bastard. I stood up with Farlan at their wedding. I'd made up my mind I'd get to traveling after the next crop came in. Go to Glasgow and seek my fortune. After I'd got Dadaigh set up for the winter.

It was shortly after Ais and Farlan's wedding that I went for a good sulk on the beach. Again, a fool age. It was a foggy day, the kind where sound travels oddly, everything seems closer and farther, and I'd heard seals barking down along the rocks. I knew this beach like I knew my own room, but today the fog was so thick I had to use the rocks as markers. I kept my hands on the cliff to the right and walked between the tidal pools to a familiar perch of an overhang that sometimes hung over sandy pebbles, other times over sea, according to the tide. I hauled myself up. The rocks were damp but there was a warm current that day and the air was comfortably warm. A clear day is where you'd freeze on this coast. I sat and squinted out at the seals when I saw her. Hair black, as black as the rocks I sat on, was woven with kelp and bracken. Her skin was the color of new cream, with rosy highlights. And her face. My goodness her face, I'd seen nothing before so bold, strong, and humorous. I can't explain why that struck me at once, but her laugh let me know I'd be in good company.

She came ashore and I shrank back behind a rock on the overhang, watching her. She was wearing nothing at all and while I had seen a naked lass before, what I saw here made me blush. She reached for her clothes and slipped them on, only things got muddled here, and it turned out it wasn't clothing at all. It was a skin. And when she had fastened it, she wasn't a human anymore at all.

I had fallen in love with a selkie.

And I knew I had two choices. Follow her into the sea and drown or the bad awful thing I did. But needs must and she was a need. And a must. And right there on the beach, I made the decision that would decide my next millennium.

LEX

There must be a reason I'm in the boat, a reason I'm here with Duncan, my best friend, and my heart for so many years. But I couldn't make any of this better. He was already dead. I hadn't stopped him from using drugs or gotten him on the wagon, He'd taken one too many pills and died. It was a stupid death. Stupider was my giving up on him so easily, but that was something I couldn't fix. We were quiet now as I rowed us forward, pulling the paddle long and slow on one side, then the other. The only sounds were the water and the immensity of the blackness above us.

He said, "I'm sorry Lex." It was echoey and his voice cracked. "I was such an asshole. I saw you every day and ducked you, avoided you. I want you to know I was like, super proud of you, being brave in the face of the stupidest age of kids."

Seventh grade was when I "came out" as non-binary. It wasn't so much coming out, my parents got it already, and it's not like I'd ever subscribed to one gender or another. It's just that I had to do the annoying thing of telling my teachers to use they/them when referring to me. Complicated when you get those old farts. And I had to deal with the kids at that time. This was after Duncan and his mom moved away. The two things weren't related. It's just that Duncan's absence was more felt at that point.

He said, "I. You had a lot going on."

I paddled, the river took us, the boat drifted a bit, perhaps giving us more time to get it sorted out. I said, "I'm sorry."

"What the hell for?"

"I didn't push. I didn't ask what was really going on with you and your mom. I think I was just too sulky about your bailing."

"We were kids, Lex. What the hell did we know about how to deal with things anyway?' He was right. He said, "What's on the other side?"

"Another tunnel. You go into the light."

He scoffed. "Ha. Total cliché."

"I guess so. I don't think it's a bad thing. Most people seem pretty cool with going through. You'll have to tell me what you feel, before you . . . " *disappear*. The word was going to be tear-filled, so I swallowed it.

"I don't want to go, Lex." His voice was so scared that it hurt to hear.

"I don't want you to go. I've missed you so much. It's. It's nice to see you again?"

He craned his neck around to look at me, "Heh. Yeah, sorta, right?"

"I miss you most Halloweens, so . . . "

"I saw you!" Like it was just dawning on him. "You were. Maaan, how gone was I?"

"You were pretty gone. But you were nice. Oh, shit, Dunk, if I'd stopped you then, if I'd dragged you back to my house. Called my mom." I wanted to. I had an overwhelming urge to. Why didn't I listen to it?

He turned around to face the river again and said, "I don't know. Maybe I'd already taken too much. Maybe that capsule just hadn't cracked open yet. You can't . . . this is on me. There's a lot on me."

"Still."

"I knew it wasn't the greatest, but once I started using, man. It just made all the Mom stuff, all the Dad stuff, sorta . . . recede you know? It seemed simpler if I didn't have to think about things."

I guess I could understand that. He could have asked for help or something though.

I said, "Dumb ways to die, right?"

We both laughed. We were obsessed with the Tangerine Kitty song in fifth grade.

Duncan started in singing it, I joined him, and it echoed into the cavern with its grim lyrics and its cheery tune. I think we both felt a little bit better for it. I wondered if this should become a routine with other folks I had to get across. Ice breaker?

DEATH

I went back to the beach the next day at the same time but did not find her. This became my quest each day and it took a fortnight until she came back. I hid while she undid her skin, hid it behind a rock, and got back into the water. I took the skin while she played and her seal friends barked, and I buried it deep in the barn under blankets in an old chest. I'd find a better place to hide it later.

I slipped out and back down to the beach hoping she wouldn't be gone. Knowing that she had nowhere to go. I brought a blanket and sure enough, I found her sitting on the beach weeping. Her friends were gone.

I put the blanket around her shoulders and comforted her as best I could. Then I brought her home.

We were married in a month, and daily she asked me for her skin. Swore she wouldn't swim away, she simply felt incomplete without it. I fobbed it off, bought her beautiful dresses, even made her a sheepskin coat as a joke one Christmas, and gave it to her wrapped, saying, "Your skin coat, m'lady." I regretted it instantly once I saw her eyes light up with hope. Of course, when she opened it and saw what it was, I realized my cruelty, but by then it was too late.

She stopped speaking to me. She took long walks down by the sea, looking out into it, at what I didn't know.

I threatened her, I pleaded with her. And after one terrible fight, where she'd said I had no right to her, I went out to the barn, and she clutched at my sleeve as I pulled out her skin and hauled it out into the night air. She begged as I threw it into a bonfire I'd laid for bracken. Dried with time, it went up in flames like it was made of straw. The wail that Maureen let loose is so deeply embedded in my bones, I won't ever be able to unhear it.

During those years of ferrying, that cry was at least kept at bay. It was too quiet in that cavern with the murmuring of lives, with the monotony, the years. Every once in a while, it itched in the back of my mind or hung like a foreboding in the blackness above the cavern. But now, looking at this cottage again, it all comes back, fresh and terrible.

The morning after I had burned the skin, Maureen was gone and that is when Danu took me to her. She had washed up down the shore by a few miles. Danu looked at me and I knew I had done the worst crime against our world. And I was condemned to the boat.

But here I am, just through the door of my household. My wife waiting by the fire. Most unnerving of all: she has a smile for me.

LEX

Duncan and I relaxed into the journey, time having left all sense. It was nice, talking about that time the family rented a beach place together down in San Clemente. We boogie boarded, got too much sun, dragged our butts up the exhausting stairs at T Street Beach, back to our cars, had too much to eat when our families cooked together, slept like logs. The more we talked, the more I was desperate to prolong the talking, to keep him with me. And the more I realized how much I'd missed him these past three, four years.

We finally, finally got to the opposite shore. I saw the shimmer of Maeve's cape before I recognized her figure standing next to the tunnel. Something like hope lifted in my chest as the boat ran ashore. I got out and went to her.

"We have to find his dad, can you help us find his dad? His mom is owed a ton of money and she doesn't have him anymore to help out. Can you help him?"

There was something all too knowing in her expression, something that wouldn't give me an inch. When she looked at me before, I always felt a surge of recognition, a thrill of being seen. But her eyes were focused only on Duncan. I hoped maybe she had heard me, that she would help.

She said, "Stay here." And she went over to Duncan, who still sat in the boat, reluctant to take that next step.

They spoke softly for a while. His voice rose only once when he said, "Do *what?*" Then she murmured at him, steadily, long, and his shoulders drooped, and he started nodding. I heard him say, "Okay. Okay, Okay."

He got out of the boat and walked past her, up to me, wordlessly. He threw his arms around me and hugged me long and hard. I wasn't going to cry. I wanted him to feel okay about moving on. He kissed me on the cheek and like that he walked into the tunnel. There was a flash of brightness I tried to peek past but said nothing. Duncan was gone and the emptiness in my chest hit me so hard I fell to my knees.

"I gotta get out of here." I got up and turned to Maeve. I said, "Can you send me home now?"

She was watching the tunnel. She said, "Wait."

We stood a long time. A forever time. I started to worry maybe there was a bigger plan. Like she'd turn me into a skeleton, or I was really dead, or something. What the hell was I doing agreeing to go with Death and some weird ass enchanted chick from the Halloween store to this place beyond? Idiot. Duncan had been so worried about his mom, and I hadn't even thought about my family. What if Maria woke up and found me gone? What would Dad think? Did I even lock the front door when I went to the front stoop? What if strangers broke in and killed everybody? Or robbed us? What if I couldn't get back and take care of everyone? I guess they'd save money on college. That'd be something. And my parents were definitely doing better than Duncan's mom who was on her last cent. But they'd miss me. I'd been worried about Dad doing Halloween next year with just Mike's help. How about under the specter of losing his oldest kid? Would Halloween be canceled? They'd always think of it as the day that Lex died. The day that . . .

There was a warm hand on my shoulder, and I turned to see Maeve. She looked at me intently and raised her hand to my forehead and pressed once firmly. There was a tingling there that passed over my head, down my shoulders, through my chest which loosened so swiftly I hadn't realized it was a knot before. My breathing slowed.

She said, "You're freaking out. This isn't about you. This is about Duncan. Wait."

And we waited. After fifteen minutes or forever, hard to tell. The light flashed again, and Duncan came out of the tunnel.

Was she giving him a second chance? Would he wake up in the morgue or something? Would he be able to go back to his life?

Maeve said, "You got it?"

He nodded. He was crying though. "I don't think I can do it."

"You know the deal."

I didn't know why that last hug had been so hard if he knew he was coming back. I said, "Can we go now?"

Maeve said, "Soon." She walked to Duncan and peered into his face. "Tell Lex."

He started toward me, and she stopped him with the palm of her hand. "You can tell them from there."

"But I. Can I at least give them another hug?"

"It's not safe for Lex if you touch them. You've been to the other side."

He wouldn't be coming back with me. Stupid idea anyway.

Duncan said, "Tell Mom he's in Vegas. The money isn't hard to get. She just needs a court order. Can you remember a number?"

"Okay."

He told me a phone number and made me repeat it four times. He then told me a street address and had me do the same.

There was this terrible horrible pause.

I said, "I'll take care of her, I promise. My dad's a lawyer, remember?"

"Thanks, Lex. Love, you, man."

Frickin' tears. "Love you."

I waited for him to turn to go but that was not what happened. Maeve stepped forward and started saying some words in a low tone, moving her hands about in front of her, sort of aimed at him.

Duncan's jacket was changing, growing? Into a robe that dropped to his feet and his body was stretching longer, taller, taller and his hair and flesh receded from his face until his skull came clear, his eyes looked at me one last time, afraid before they receded as well, and he became Death.

I said, "Wait, what the hell?"

Maeve said, "No, not exactly."

"What did you do?" This was all wrong. You can't just change people into Charon. It's not cool. I marched over to her, my feet crunching on the gravely sand on the shore. I was taller than her. "You turn him back. You can't do that."

She said, "He agreed."

"Agreed to what exactly?"

She said, "He did a bad thing. This is one way to pay. The other way would be much less pleasant, believe me."

He didn't look afraid. Not that he had an expression to read anymore. But I think I'd know if he was afraid. He simply stood, waiting, next to the boat. I felt his presence missing as acutely as I had when he first went through that tunnel, as I had when he ghosted me that summer.

Ghosted.

I said, "This. This is horrible. What can he possibly have done to deserve this?"

Maeve's gaze did not waver. She said only, "That is not your story."

And got in the boat. She motioned to the seat next to her. I didn't want to sit anywhere near her. But when Duncan got into the boat. Death, for that, is now what he was, I followed. I didn't want to be trapped here. I had to help his mom. I'd promised.

As we got to the other side and stepped out of the boat, I saw a redheaded man coming through the tunnel. He had tears in his eyes and an odd, distant look on his face. I recognized it from those

I'd gotten across so far, but there was something familiar about this guy. In his stance, in his cheekbones. He saw Maeve and smiled weakly at her before he approached the boat. He looked at Death, and then looked back at Maeve with a question.

She said, "You can go now. Time to move on."

Relief flooded over the man's body and his shoulders fell, but his face lightened. As Maeve and I walked through the tunnel I could swear I felt Duncan look back at me one more time. But as I looked over my shoulder there was nothing there but blackness, and things went fuzzy and I woke up in my bed, in my suit, my boots still on. Maybe it was all a horrible very vivid dream. Right? I mean, right? *Please, God, let it be a dream.* But when I slung my legs over to hit the floor there was a bit of a crunch. I reached down and grabbed a clump of mud clinging to my boot. It was black, shiny, elemental like on the beach of the river.

I looked at my phone. It was already seven. I immediately opened my memos and typed in the number and address Duncan had made me memorize. Then I sent myself an email just to be safe. I made my way into the kitchen where I found Dad fumbling around with some pancake batter. I threw my arms around his shoulders and hugged, maybe too hard. I said, "Dad, you don't have to make breakfast." I knew he was nursing a pretty major hangover.

He laughed. "Happy All Saint's Day. All Saint's Day we have pancakes."

I said, "Coffee?"

"Yes, please."

The detritus of Halloween surrounded us, two shriveled fingers in a blanket lay wrapped in a dishtowel in a basket on the counter. Countless dirty glasses littered the sink, and the trash can was stuffed with all kinds of garbage.

I instantly thought of Duncan's mom, waking up to the worst news of her life. Maeve had told me to wait a few weeks to talk to her. Let her do what she needed to do grief-wise. But. Oh God. I mean I knew of his loss in that space in the dark, I knew he was dead on the boat, but in this Halloween littered kitchen with that first sugar tinge of pancakes cooking, I felt I was getting the news all over again.

And then as if I'd willed it, my mom came into the kitchen with a stricken look on her face, her phone in her hand. She said, "Honey, change into your clothes. We've got to go."

I didn't have to act too hard that I was just getting the news, because the actual news in the cold hard light of day hurt as bad as the first time I saw him come through that tunnel. When we went to his apartment and his mom, Molly's face was swollen and twisted from crying, I knew that no amount of money was going to make up for the fact that Duncan was gone.

Things happened pretty quickly. At Duncan's funeral, Molly had me speak. His miscreant friends were there looking quite taken aback. Their parents flanked them like guards. Someone had gotten in a lot of trouble.

Molly did find her ex, and with the help of a lawyer and an arrest, got some of that money back. She used some of it to found an after-school program for kids. I hate that she blamed herself for what happened when it was clearly her stinking ex and Charlie who'd driven Duncan down that path, but you can't help how someone feels about something that's happened to them. There was some satisfaction in helping Duncan get what he wanted done. But nothing was ever going to make what happened that Halloween night okay.

It was only five years later that I ran into Charlie at the Galleria at Christmastime where he was working security. He told me that he and Duncan had gotten some supplies, made a batch of pills, and sold them. It never got traced back to them, but I realized around Halloween that year there were a string of ODs among kids our age. I guess that was the *not your story* that I'd wondered about. Duncan wasn't a *bad person*. You know? It seems like only a bad person would have to make that kind of choice. Charlie had gotten clean. Their other friend Stuart hadn't and was doing time upstate for dealing. This was life. One little wrong step, one bad decision, and things could just go sideways.

I don't know how long Duncan has, but there's an odd part of me that wants him there when it's my turn to cross. But that won't be until after a very long time.

The week after that Halloween night, I got the suit dry cleaned since there was mud on the ankles of it, and I dragged my feet a week before bringing it back to *Halloween Beyond*. I blamed it on the funeral, all the goings-on, but the truth was, I didn't want to go. Didn't like the idea of being near Maeve again. I don't care what Duncan did, what she did was a mean trick.

Dad said, "Look, it's a great suit. If they fine you, I'm happy to pay it." He knew how ridiculous these places could be.

I both wanted and didn't want to see Maeve. I'd probably want to kill her. I reminded myself she didn't kill Duncan. She did something else. Something worse.

We pulled up to the storefront, but the sign was gone as were the window dressings. I figured they were just cleaning up for the year, but when I got to the front door and pressed my face against the glass, it was obvious shop had been abandoned. There was an envelope taped to the front door with a ridiculously gorgeous *Lex* drawn on it with what looked like a quill. I opened the envelope.

It read: *The suit is yours, as it always has been. That was you out there. You need no excuses or answers. You can just be.* Nothing else, just a signature of a flourished M.

I shoved the envelope in my pocket and carried the suit back to the car where Dad was on Words with Friends. He looked up as I approached and rolled down the window. "What, they closed?"

I hung the suit in the back seat and got in the car.

"They're gone." I said.

"Gone?"

"For good."

"Huh." Dad pulled away from the curb and in about a block he started to chuckle.

I said, "What?"

He said, "Halloween . . . *Beyond*." His laugh turned to a cackle as we headed up the hill toward home.

THE END?

Not if you want to dive into more of Crystal Lake Publishing's Tales from the Darkest Depths!

Check out our amazing website and online store
or download our latest catalog here.

We always have great new projects and content on the website to dive into, as well as a newsletter, behind the scenes options, social media platforms, our own dark fiction shared-world series and our very own webstore. If you use the IGotMyCLPBook! coupon code in the store (at the checkout), you'll get a one-time-only 50% discount on your first eBook purchase!

Our webstore even has categories specifically for KU books, non-fiction, anthologies, and of course more novels and novellas.

Subscribe to Crystal Lake Publishing's Dark Tide series for updates, specials, behind-the-scenes content, and a special selection of bonus stories - http://eepurl.com/hKVGkr

ABOUT THE AUTHORS

Lisa Morton is a screenwriter, author of non-fiction books, and prose writer whose work was described by the American Library Association's *Readers' Advisory Guide to Horror* as "consistently dark, unsettling, and frightening." She is a six-time winner of the Bram Stoker Award®, the author of four novels and over 150 short stories, and a world-class Halloween and paranormal expert. Her recent releases include *Haunted Tales: Classic Stories of Ghosts and the Supernatural* (co-edited with Leslie S. Klinger), and *Calling the Spirits: A History of Seances*. Lisa lives in Los Angeles and online at www.lisamorton.com .

Lucy A. Snyder is the Shirley Jackson Award-nominated and five-time Bram Stoker Award-winning author of 15 books and over 100 published short stories. Her most recent books are the poetry collection *Exposed Nerves* and the forthcoming novel *Sister, Maiden, Monsterl*. She also wrote the novels *Spellbent, Shotgun Sorceress*, and *Switchblade Goddess*, the nonfiction book *Shooting Yourself in the Head for Fun and Profit: A Writer's Survival Guide*, and the collections *Halloween Season, Garden of Eldritch Delights, While the Black Stars Burn, Soft Apocalypses, Orchid Carousals, Sparks and Shadows, Chimeric Machines*, and *Installing Linux on a Dead Badger*. Her writing has been translated into French, Russian, Italian, Spanish, Czech, and Japanese editions and has appeared in publications such as *Asimov's Science Fiction, Apex Magazine, Nightmare Magazine, Pseudopod, Strange Horizons*, and *Best Horror of the Year*. She lives in Ohio with a jungle of houseplants, a clowder of cats, and an insomnia of housemates. You can learn more about her at www.lucysnyder.com and you can follow her on Twitter at @LucyASnyder.

Kate Maruyama's novel *Harrowgate* was published by 47North and her novella, *Family Solstice*, named Best Fiction Book of 2021 by *Rue Morgue Magazine* is out now from Omnium Gatherum. Her short work has appeared in *Asimov's Magazine, Analog SF,* and other journals and in numerous anthologies including *December Tales* and *Halloween Carnival Three*. She writes, teaches, cooks, and eats in Los Angeles.

Crystal Lake Publishing's most popular anthologies:

Readers . . .

Thank you for reading *Halloween Beyond*. We hope you enjoyed this 4th book in our Dark Tide series.

If you have a moment, please review *Halloween Beyond* at the store where you bought it.

Help other readers by telling them why you enjoyed this book. No need to write an in-depth discussion. Even a single sentence will be greatly appreciated. Reviews go a long way to helping a book sell, and is great for an author's career. It'll also help us to continue publishing quality books. You can also share a photo of yourself holding this book with the hashtag #IGotMyCLPBook!

Thank you again for taking the time to journey with Crystal Lake Publishing.

Visit our Linktree page for a list of our social media platforms.
https://linktr.ee/CrystalLakePublishing

Our Mission Statement:

Since its founding in August 2012, Crystal Lake Publishing has quickly become one of the world's leading publishers of Dark Fiction and Horror books in print, eBook, and audio formats.

While we strive to present only the highest quality fiction and entertainment, we also endeavour to support authors along their writing journey. We offer our time and experience in non-fiction projects, as well as author mentoring and services, at competitive prices.

With several Bram Stoker Award wins and many other wins and nominations (including the HWA's Specialty Press Award), Crystal Lake Publishing puts integrity, honor, and respect at the forefront of our publishing operations.

We strive for each book and outreach program we spearhead to not only entertain and touch or comment on issues that affect our readers, but also to strengthen and support the Dark Fiction field and its authors.

Not only do we find and publish authors we believe are destined for greatness, but we strive to work with men and woman who endeavour to be decent human beings who care more for others than themselves, while still being hard working, driven, and passionate artists and storytellers.

Crystal Lake Publishing is and will always be a beacon of what passion and dedication, combined with overwhelming teamwork and respect, can accomplish. We endeavour to know each and every one of our readers, while building personal relationships with our authors, reviewers, bloggers, podcasters, bookstores, and libraries.

We will be as trustworthy, forthright, and transparent as any business can be, while also keeping most of the headaches away from our authors, since it's our job to solve the problems so they can stay in a creative mind. Which of course also means paying our authors.

We do not just publish books, we present to you worlds within your world, doors within your mind, from talented authors who sacrifice so much for a moment of your time.

There are some amazing small presses out there, and through collaboration and open forums we will continue to support other presses in the goal of helping authors and showing the world what quality small presses are capable of accomplishing. No one wins when a small press goes down, so we will always be there to support hardworking, legitimate presses and their authors. We don't see Crystal Lake as the best press out there, but we will always strive to be the best, strive to be the most interactive and grateful, and even blessed press around. No matter what happens over time, we will also take our mission very seriously while appreciating where we are and enjoying the journey.

What do we offer our authors that they can't do for themselves through self-publishing?

We are big supporters of self-publishing (especially hybrid publishing), if done with care, patience, and planning. However, not every author has the time or inclination to do market research, advertise, and set up book launch strategies. Although a lot of authors are successful in doing it all, strong small presses will always be there for the authors who just want to do what they do best: write.

What we offer is experience, industry knowledge, contacts and trust built up over years. And due to our strong brand and trusting fanbase, every Crystal Lake Publishing book comes with weight of respect. In time our fans begin to trust our judgment and will try a new author purely based on our support of said author.

With each launch we strive to fine-tune our approach, learn from our mistakes, and increase our reach. We continue to assure our authors that we're here for them and that we'll carry the weight of the launch and dealing with third parties while they focus on their strengths—be it writing, interviews, blogs, signings, etc.

We also offer several mentoring packages to authors that include knowledge and skills they can use in both traditional and self-publishing endeavours.

We look forward to launching many new careers.

This is what we believe in. What we stand for. This will be our legacy.

Welcome to Crystal Lake Publishing—
Tales from the Darkest Depths.